Maria Reva was born ... an MFA from the Michener Centre for ... the University of Texas. Her fiction has appeared in the *Atlantic*, *McSweeney's*, *Best American Short Stories* and elsewhere, and has won a National Magazine Award. She also works as an opera librettist.

'Bright, funny, satirical and relevant ... A new talent to watch!'
Margaret Atwood (from Twitter)

'Creative, poignant and darkly hilarious, *Good Citizens Need Not Fear* is full of relevant questions about resistance, corruption and maintaining dignity against the dehumanizing power of the State. This is an outstanding first book'
Anthony Doerr, author of *All the Light We Cannot See*

'*Good Citizens Need Not Fear* is the funniest, most politically astute book I've read in years. Reva's pitch perfect tone – especially at that comic junction where the absurdity of a system rigged to control human beings collides with actual humans – is bang-on brilliant'
Miriam Toews, author of *Women Talking*

'Maria Reva's enthralling debut of interlinked short stories achieves the double effect of timelessness and timeliness. The emotional impact of this book is cumulative. This is partly down to her mastery of the form: the stories are connected by a unity of place, time and relationship. More importantly, they are brought to life by Reva's handling of darkness and light'
Kapka Kassabova, *Guardian*

'Luminous. These stories speak with humour yet real emotion of the heaviness of totalitarian systems and show how the light of our humanity
Yann Mart

GOOD CITIZENS NEED *not* FEAR

MARIA REVA

virago

VIRAGO

First published in the United States in 2020 by Doubleday
First published in Great Britain in 2020 by Virago Press
This paperback edition published in 2021 by Virago Press

13 5 7 9 10 8 6 4 2

Several stories originally appeared, some in slightly different form, in
the following publications: 'Novostroïka' in *The Atlantic* (December 2016);
'Little Rabbit' as 'Unsound' in *McSweeney's Quarterly Concern* (August 2018);
'Letter of Apology' in *Granta* (November 2018); and 'The Ermine Coat'
published by the Writers' Trust of Canada and winner of the
RBC Bronwen Wallace Award in 2018.

A CIP catalogue record for this book is available from the British Library.

ISBN 978-0-349-01268-1

Book design by Maria Carella
Printed and bound in Great Britain by Clays Ltd, Elcograf S.p.A.

Papers used by Virago are from well-managed forests
and other responsible sources.

Virago Press
An imprint of
Little, Brown Book Group
Carmelite House
50 Victoria Embankment
London EC4Y 0DZ

An Hachette UK Company
www.hachette.co.uk

www.virago.co.uk

To my family

CONTENTS

PART ONE

Before the Fall

PART TWO

After the Fall

PART
ONE

Before
the
Fall

NOVOSTROÏKA

The statue of Grandfather Lenin, just like the one in Moscow, 900 kilometers away, squinted into the smoggy distance. Winter's first snowflakes settled on its iron shoulders like dandruff. Even as Daniil Petrovich Blinov passed the statue and climbed the crumbling steps of the town council behind it, he felt the Grandfather's 360-degree gaze on the back of his head, burning through his fur-flap hat.

Inside the town council hall, a line of hunched figures pressed against the walls, warming their hands on the radiators. Men, women, entire families progressed toward a wall of glass partitions. Daniil entered the line. He rocked back and forth on the sides of his feet. When his heels grew numb, he flexed his calves to promote circulation.

"Next!"

Daniil took a step forward. He bent down to the hole in the partition and looked at the bespectacled woman sitting behind it. "I'm here to report a heating problem in our building."

"What's the problem?"

"We have no heat." He explained that the building was a new one, this winter was its first, someone seemed to have forgotten to connect it to the district furnace, and the toilet water froze at night.

The clerk heaved a thick directory onto her counter. "Building address?"

"Ivansk Street, Number 1933."

She flipped through the book, licking her finger every few pages. She flipped and flipped, consulted an index, flipped once more, shut the book, and folded her arms across it. "That building does not exist, Citizen."

Daniil stared at the woman. "What do you mean? I live there."

"According to the documentation, you do not." The clerk looked over Daniil's shoulder at the young couple in line behind him.

Daniil leaned closer, too quickly, banging his forehead against the partition. "Nineteen thirty-three Ivansk Street," he repeated, enunciating each syllable.

"Never heard of it."

"I have thirteen, no, fourteen people living in my suite alone, who can come here and tell you all about it," Daniil said. "Fourteen angry citizens bundled up to twice their size."

The clerk shook her head, tapped the book. "The documentation, Citizen."

"We'll keep using the gas, then. We'll leave the stove on day and night." The stove offered little in the way of heating, but Daniil hoped the wanton waste of a government-subsidized resource would stir a response.

The woman raised her eyebrows; Daniil appeared to have rematerialized in front of her. "Address again?"

"Nineteen thirty-three Ivansk Street, Kirovka, Ukraine, USSR. Mother Earth."

"Yes, yes. We'll have the gas-engineering department look into it. Next!"

—

Was it fourteen now? Had he included himself in the count? Carefully avoiding the ice patches on the sidewalk on his way home, Daniil wondered when he had let the numbers elude him. Last month twelve people had been living in his suite, including himself. He counted on his fingers, stiff from the cold. In the bedroom, first corner, Baba Ola slept on the foldout armchair; second corner, on the foldout cot, were Aunt Inaya and Uncle Timko and their three small children (but Uncle Timko promised they'd be assigned their own place soon because of his job superintending the municipal square's public restroom— a government position); third corner, Daniil's niece and her friend, but they hardly counted, since they ate little and spent most of their time at the institute; fourth corner, Daniil himself, bunking under Uncle Timko's mother, (Great) Aunt Nika; in the hallway, someone's mother-in-law or second cousin or who really knew, the connection was patchy; on the balcony camped Second Cousin Glebik and his fiancée and six hens, which were not included in the count but who could forget the damn noisy birds? That made thirteen. He must have missed someone.

Daniil's name had bounced from wait list to wait list for three years before he'd been assigned to his apartment by the Kirovka Canning Combine, where he worked as a packaging specialist. The ten-story paneled *novostroïka* was newly built and still smelled of mortar. His fifth-floor suite was no larger than the single room he had shared with his parents in a communal apartment, but he could call it his own. The day he'd moved in had been nothing short of sublime: he'd walked to his sink, filled a glass of water, guzzled it down, then lay on the kitchen floor with his legs squeezed into the gap between the stove and table. Home was where one could lie in peace, on any surface. He felt fresh and full of hope. Then came a knock at the door. Daniil's grandmother burst into the apartment, four mildewy sacks of grain and a cage full of hens strapped to her back. She spoke Ukrainian, which Daniil barely understood, having been raised and educated in Russian. She cursed her neighbor, who either was in love with her or had it in for her and had threatened to poison himself, or her, or perhaps both. Daniil simply nodded, ashamed to ask for clarification. And so Baba Ola stayed.

Two. Two had been fine. Until two became fourteen.

—

Minimum Dimensions of Space Necessary for Human Functioning, 85 processes: Sleeping (based on average Moscow male, head to toe) = 175 cm. Standing (gravitational effect included) = 174.5 cm. Opening oven (based on average Moscow female, buttocks to baking tray) = 63.5 cm. Washing face (elbow to elbow) = 52 cm. Opening refrigerator (door span area) = $\pi(55 \text{ cm})^2 \div 4$. Lacing up boots (floor space) = 63.5 cm x 43 cm. Pulling out dining chair (floor space) = 40 cm x 40 cm. Mending clothing, shoes, other (floor space) = 40 cm x 40 cm. Child rearing (floor space for corner time) = 30 cm x 30 cm. Watching educational television programs = 64.5 cm x 40 cm. Listening to educational radio programs = 64.5 cm x 40 cm. Evacuating bladder (volume) = 400 ml. Mental training (based on average Moscow male, brain volume) = 1260 cm^3. Dreaming = 1260 cm^3 ... or ∞? Breathing (torso expansion) = 1.5 cm. Yawning (torso expansion) = 3 cm. Sneezing (torso retraction) = 3–4 cm.

Stretching (limb extension) = n/a. Etc. Etc. Minimum dimensions necessary for human functioning (TOTAL) = 9 m^2.

—

Daniil stuffed his hands back into the damp warmth of his pockets as he climbed the narrow set of stairs to his floor.

Suite 56 greeted him with its familiar smell, boiled potatoes and fermenting cabbage. "Daniil, is that you?" Aunt Nika hollered from the kitchen. At sixty-five, her voice retained its cutting timbre, perfectly suited for her job hawking seed oils at the bazaar. "Come look, we get barely any gas."

Daniil cringed. He had wanted to remain unnoticed by his relatives for a few seconds longer. When he opened the closet to hang his coat, a pair of gray eyes stared back at him, round and unblinking. Daniil started. He had forgotten Grandfather Grishko, who slept standing, as he used to do while guarding a military museum in Kiev. This was the fourteenth member of the Blinov residence. Daniil closed the door softly.

"Took me three hours to boil potatoes," Aunt Nika told Daniil when he stepped into the kitchen. She wore a stained apron over a floor-length mink coat inherited from her grandmother. Its massive hood obscured her face. She turned the knobs to maximum; the burner heads quivered with a faint blue. "Did you go to the town council? They should look into it."

"It seems they already have," Daniil said. "But they're better at turning things off than on."

A pigtailed girl, Aunt Inaya and Uncle Timko's, jumped out from under the kitchen table singing, "May there always be sunshine / May there always be blue skies." She air-fired at the lightbulb hanging from the ceiling. Aunt Nika gently scratched the nape of the girl's neck, and the child retreated back under the table.

"What did they tell you at the council?" Aunt Nika asked.

"The building doesn't exist, and we don't live here."

Aunt Nika's mittened hand brushed a strand of dyed red hair off her forehead. "Makes sense."

"How so?"

"I had a talk with the benchers last week." She meant the group of pensioners who sat at the main entrance of the building, ever vigilant, smoking unfiltered cigarettes and cracking sunflower seeds day and night. "They told me this block was supposed to have only two towers, but enough construction material had been discarded to cobble together a third—ours."

A series of barks blasted through the thin walls of the bedroom. Daniil glanced in alarm at Aunt Nika. He hadn't approved of the hens, but they were at least useful—now a dog?

Aunt Nika cast her eyes down. "Vovik. Bronchitis again, poor boy. What are you going to do about the gas?"

Aunt Nika's granddaughter bellowed from under the table, "May there always be mother / May there always be me!"

"I don't know," said Daniil.

Uncle Timko appeared in the doorway to announce that he needed a glass of milk. Daniil and Aunt Nika evacuated the kitchen and waited in the hallway while he opened the refrigerator.

The human shuffle complete, Daniil resumed inspecting the stove. Aunt Nika followed, her fur hood falling over her eyes until she flung it off, releasing a cloud of dust.

"Grandfather Grishko's telling everyone he hasn't seen

his own testicles in weeks," she said. "We're tired of the cold, Daniil."

As if in agreement, Vovik's coughing started up again, deeper in pitch, as though it came not from the bedroom but from beneath the floor. Daniil couldn't imagine the dainty four-year-old producing such sounds. He stroked the smooth enamel of the stove, never having felt so useless.

"And we're tired of hearing about the testicles."

The memo on Daniil's desk the next morning unsettled him. It was addressed from Moscow:

> In accordance with General Assembly No. 3556 of the Ministry of Food Industry, Ministry of Meat and Dairy Industry, and Ministry of Fish Industry on January 21, 1985, the Kirovka Canning Combine has been ordered to economize 2.5 tons of tinplate per month, due to shortages. Effective immediately.

At the bottom of the memo, his superior's blockish hand-writing:

THIS MEANS YOU, BLINOV.

The telephone on his desk rang.

"You've read the memo?" It was Sergei Igorovich, his superior, calling. Daniil turned to look across many rows of desks. Sergei Igorovich stood in the doorway of his office, receiver pressed to his ear, watching Daniil.

"I have, Sergei Igorovich."

Daniil went on to inquire about testing alternative tin-to-steel ratios for containers.

"None of that, Blinov. Just stuff more food into fewer cans. Use every cubic millimeter you have," his superior said. "I see that you're not writing this down."

Daniil pulled up an old facsimile and set about doodling big-eared Cheburashka, a popular cartoon creature unknown to science.

"Good, very good," Sergei Igorovich said. "But don't think of pureeing anything."

"No?"

"The puree machine's on its way to Moscow. Commissar's wife just had twins."

Daniil examined the diameter of Cheburashka's head, making sure the ears matched its size. "Sergei Igorovich? May I ask you something?"

"If it's quick."

"I was looking over the impressive list of goods our combine produces, and couldn't help wondering—where does it all go?"

"Is that a philosophical question, Blinov?"

"All I see in stores is sea cabbage."

Sergei Igorovich let out a long sigh. "It's like that joke about the American, the Frenchman, and the Soviet guy."

"I haven't heard that one, Sergei Igorovich."

"A shame," Sergei Igorovich said. "When I have time to paint my nails and twiddle my thumbs, I'll tell you the joke."

Daniil resisted the temptation to roll himself into a defensive ball under his desk, like a hedgehog. He straightened his shoulders. "Sergei Igorovich? May I also ask about the pay."

Daniil watched his superior retreat into his office, mumbling into his phone about the shortages. Surely the pay would come through next month, Sergei Igorovich said, and if not then, the month after, and in the meantime don't ask too many questions. He hung up.

Daniil reached into his desk drawer, extracting a new sheet of graph paper and a T-square. He ran his fingers over the instrument, rich red, made of wild pearwood. When he was a child, his parents had awarded him the T-square for top marks in school. At the time, he'd thought the pearwood held some magical property, a secret promise.

He set to work drawing diagrams of food products in 400-milliliter cylinders. Chains of equations filled his graph paper. Some foods posed more of a packing problem than others: pickles held their shape, for instance, while tomatoes had near-infinite squeezability. Soups could be thickened and condensed milk condensed further, into a mortar-like substance. String beans proved the most difficult: Even when arranged like a honeycomb, they could reach only 91 percent packing efficiency. In the middle of every three string beans hid an unfillable space. By lunchtime, Daniil had submitted a report titled "The Problematics of the String-Bean Triangular Void" to Sergei Igorovich's secretary.

For the rest of the day, Daniil pretended to work while the combine pretended to pay him. He drew Gena the Crocodile, Cheburashka's sidekick. He pondered the properties of dandruff, specifically Grandfather Lenin's dandruff. Could a bald man have dandruff? Unlikely. What, then, about the goatee?

—

Canning for civilian consumption: sausages in pork fat sausages in tomato sauce kidneys in tomato sauce hearts in tomato sauce roast brains roast pork and rice pressed meat liver paste tongue in jelly fried meat macaroni with beef pork or mutton beans peas with beef pork or mutton meat pies sweet and sour meat mixed offals udder liver heart kidneys head cheek tail ends and trimmings fat salt onions plus one bay leaf whitefish in vegetable oil sturgeon in vegetable oil with the occasional bone to be retracted from esophagus in one of many district clinics available to citizens mackerel in vegetable oil fried red mullet in vegetable oil sheatfish in vegetable oil sprats in vegetable oil pike perch in vegetable oil plaice in vegetable oil sardines in vegetable oil bream in vegetable oil goby in vegetable oil sturgeon in natural juice of the fish salmon in natural juice of the fish Caspian roach in natural juice of the fish whale meat in natural juice of the mammal anchovies in vinegar sprats in vinegar sardines in vinegar also in fish cakes ground or mixed in vegetables tuna cod crab carp caviar sliced eggplant vegetable marrow sliced vegetables tomato puree tomato paste tomato catsup pureed sorrel pureed beet plus one bay leaf green peas in natural juice of the legume asparagus in natural juice of the vegetable cauliflower in natural juice of the vegetable beets in natural juice of the vegetable carrots in natural juice of the vegetable sliced eggplant in tomato sauce with vegetable oil eggplant paste in tomato sauce with vegetable oil pepper and tomato in tomato sauce with vegetable oil eggplant and squash in tomato sauce with vegetable oil vegetable marrow in tomato sauce with vegetable oil sliced vegetables in tomato sauce with vegetable oil tomato puree tomato paste tomato catsup spinach puree sorrel puree red pepper puree green pea puree beet puree carrot puree vegetable soup puree vegetable marrow vegetable marrow stuffed with rice vegetable marrow in tomato to lower national risk of gastrointestinal disease sliced apricots in natural juice of the fruit sliced apples in natural juice of the fruit apricots in sugar syrup quince in sugar syrup grapes in sugar syrup cherries in sugar syrup pears in sugar syrup raisins in sugar syrup apricots pureed pears pureed peaches pureed plums pureed apples pureed for the toothless young and old condensed and dried milk constitute the most common canned milk products cylindrical oval rectangular pyramidal cans are packed in wooden boxes made of dry wood with a water content of not over 18 percent and if one or all of the above food products is unavailable: potatoes

—

Daniil reached the entrance to his building in late evening. His eyelids were heavy with fatigue, but his feet resisted going inside. Perhaps it was the hacking coughs, the endless questions, the innumerable pairs of shoes he'd have to dig through just to find his slippers. With his index finger he traced the red stenciled numbers and letters beside the main entrance. Nineteen thirty-three Ivansk Street. The building was a clone of the other two buildings on the block: identical panels, square windows, and metal entrances; identical wear in the mortar; identical rebar under the balconies, leaching rust. Nineteen thirty-three Ivansk was solidly there, in front of his nose. He blinked. But if it wasn't? He stepped closer to the stenciled numbers, felt the cold breath of the concrete. Was he the only one who could see it? It was there. Or it wasn't.

"Fudgy Cow?" a voice behind him asked.

Daniil jumped, and turned. He discerned the hunched silhouette of one of the benchers. From the spot the man occupied—right bench, left armrest—he knew it was Pyotr Palashkin, retired English teacher, loyal Voice of America listener. Palashkin lit a cigarette, illuminating his mole-specked face, and handed a candy to Daniil. The chubby cow on the paper wrapper smiled up at him dreamily. Daniil hadn't seen candy like this for months. He pocketed it for later.

"What are you out here stroking the wall for?" Palashkin asked.

Daniil shrugged. "I was just on my way in." He stayed put.

Palashkin looked up at the sky. He said in a low voice, "It's all going to collapse, you know."

"Oh?"

"Whispers are all we hear now, rumors here and there, but give it a few more years. Know what I'm saying? It's all going kaput."

Daniil gave the concrete wall a pat. "Let's just hope none of us are inside when she goes."

"What are you, cuckoo in the head? We're already inside. And I'm not talking about that building."

"I don't know about you, but I'm outside," Daniil said, now feeling unsure.

"Go eat your Fudgy Cow, Daniil." Palashkin extinguished his cigarette between his thumb and his index finger, stood up, and disappeared into the dark.

Daniil bent so close to the glass partition, he could almost curl his lips through the circular opening. The woman in booth number 7 (booths 1 to 6 were CLOSED FOR TECHNICAL BREAK), Kirovka Department of Gas, wore a fuzzy yellow sweater that Daniil found comforting, even inviting. He gazed at her and felt a twinge of hope.

The woman shut the directory with a thud. "What was it, 1933 Petrovsk, you said?"

"Ivansk."

"Look, I've heard rumors about that place, but it's not on any of the lists. Nineteen thirty-three Petrovsk is, though."

"That doesn't help me."

"Don't be hostile, Citizen. You are one of many, and I work alone."

"I know you know 1933 Ivansk exists. It exists enough for you to fiddle with the gas when you feel like it," Daniil said.

"What are you accusing us of, exactly?"

"Us? I thought you worked alone."

The woman took off her reading glasses, rubbed the bridge of her nose. "Refer to the town council with your questions."

"Already did. They said you'd fix it."

"Refer to the factory in charge of your suite assignment."

"What do they know? The whole combine is in a state of panic." Daniil was referring to the problem of the string bean.

"Best wishes with your heating problem," the woman pronounced. "Next!"

—

Candies Available for Civilian Consumption: Masha and Bear / Bear in the North / Little Bear / Clumsy Bear / Stratosphere / Strike! / Brighter! / Little Squirrel / Thumbelina / Moscow in Evening / Kiev in Evening / Fantastic Bird / Little Lemon / Little Lenin / Snowflake / Jelly / Fuzzy / Iris / Fudgy Cow / Little Red Hat / Alyonka / Little Miracle / Solidarity / Leningrad / Bird's Milk / Red Poppy / Mask / Meteorite / Vizit / Red Moscow / Dream / Caramel Crab Necks / Goose Feet / Duck Beaks / Kiss Kiss / Golden Key / Snow / Crazy Bee . . . And So Many More!

—

Daniil entered his apartment to find every square centimeter of shelf and bed space covered in stacks of red bills. His relatives had squeezed themselves into corners to count the money.

Daniil backed out of the apartment, closed the door behind him, stood on the landing until he had counted to thirty, and reentered. The red bills were still there. All right, he thought, so the hallucination continues. Run with it. Let the mind have its fancy.

The children's shrieks and snivels and coughs rang out from the kitchen, yet seemed warped and far away, as though they were coming from inside a tunnel.

Uncle Timko, the only grown-up not counting bills, sat cross-legged on Daniil's bunk, hacking away at a block of wood with a mallet and chisel. "Your grandfather's disappearing testicles saved the day, Daniil," he said, without looking up.

"I can't stand lamenting them anymore," said Grandfather Grishko, cocooned in a comforter. "Back in my district, they enjoyed quite a reputation. The girls would come from far and wide—" He went on to say a few things Daniil chose to expunge from his hallucination.

"The *children!*" Aunt Nika exclaimed from the depths of her fur.

Grandfather Grishko tossed a red stack at Daniil, and Daniil leafed through the crisp bills, half-expecting them to crackle and burst into pyrotechnic stars.

"This is my life's savings, Daniil," his grandfather said. "I've been keeping it for hard times, and hard times have arrived. Take the money. Don't ask me where I've been stashing it. Put it in for heating, bribe someone—anything."

Daniil mustered a weak thank-you.

Uncle Timko held up his mangled block of wood. "Does this look like a spoon or a toothpick?"

"Neither."

"It's supposed to be both."

"You're getting wood chips all over my sheets," protested Daniil.

Uncle Timko ignored him. "Spoon on one end, toothpick on the other. A basic instrument of survival."

When at last the counting was done, Grandfather Grishko's savings, along with money the other relatives had scrounged up, came to a hefty 8,752 rubles and 59 kopeks.

Daniil did a quick calculation in his head, imagining what 8,752 rubles and 59 kopeks could buy. He took the rabid inflation into account, and recalled the prices he'd seen at the half-empty state store the week before. Then he looked up from the stacks of bills into the expectant eyes of his family.

"We've got enough here to buy one space heater," he declared. He quickly held up a cautionary finger to stop the dreamers in the room. "If I can find one."

The next day, Daniil found another memo on his desk, this one from Sergei Igorovich:

TO FILL UNFILLABLE STRING-BEAN TRIANGULAR VOID,
ENGINEER TRIANGULAR VEGETABLE.
DUE FRIDAY.

Daniil rubbed his temples. An irresistible desire to stretch came over him. He wanted his body to fill the office, his arms and legs to stick out of the doors and windows. He wanted to leap and gambol where wild pearwood grew. His great parachute lungs would inflate, sucking up all the air on the planet.

The phone rang.

Sergei Igorovich was calling from his office again. He stood in his doorway, coiling the powder-blue phone cable around his index finger. "Is that a Fudgy Cow on your desk?"

"Just the wrapper, Sergei Igorovich."

"I haven't had one in months."

The line filled with heavy silence.

"I should get back to the triangular vegetable, Sergei Igorovich."

"You should." Sergei Igorovich kept the receiver pressed to his ear. "Blinov?"

"Yes, Sergei Igorovich."

"Was it good?"

"The candy? A bit stale."

Sergei Igorovich let out a brief moan before glancing over at his own superior's office, to find that he was being observed as well. He hung up.

Daniil placed the wrapper in his drawer, beside the T-square and his drawings of the Cheburashka gang. He turned to the diagram lying on his desk: a tin can containing exactly seventeen black olives. Seventeen was the maximum capacity, provided the olives were a constant size. The ones in the middle compacted into cubes, with barely any space for brine. Good, thought Daniil. No one drinks the brine anyway.

The heater was set to a lavish High. Its amber power light flickered like a campfire. Fourteen figures huddled around the rattling tin box and took turns allowing the warm air to tickle their faces. A few disrobed down to their sweaters. A bottle of *samogon* appeared from its hiding place, as did a can of sprats. Daniil felt warmth spread to his toes, to his chilliest spots. Aunt Nika took off her hood; her cheeks had gained a lively red. Grandfather Grishko sat on a stool like a king, knees spread, about to bite into a piece of *vobla* jerky he claimed predated the Great October Revolution.

"Let's hope the jerky has fared better than Ukraine," toasted Aunt Nika.

A knock came at the door.

Everyone fell quiet.

Another knock.

Aunt Nika poked Daniil's arm.

Daniil took another swig of home brew, slid off his chair (which Uncle Timko immediately occupied), and opened the door.

Two tall men in black beanies stood in the narrow hallway, holding a coffin.

Daniil felt himself teeter as his relatives crowded behind him. "If you're here to collect me, I'm not ready yet."

"We need access to your apartment, Citizen," the square-jawed man on the right said.

"Why?" Daniil asked.

The man on the left, endowed with wet meaty lips, rolled his eyes at his colleague. "God dammit, Petya, do we have to give an explanation at every landing?"

"An explanation would be nice," Daniil insisted.

"The guy on ninth croaked, and the stair landings aren't wide enough to pivot the coffin," Petya said. "So we need to do it inside the apartments."

"Yet somehow you got it all the way up to ninth." Daniil knew the cabinet-size elevator wouldn't have been an option.

"When the coffin was empty, we could turn it upright."

"And now you can't."

Petya narrowed his eyes at Daniil. "Some might find that disrespectful, Citizen." In agreement, Baba Ola flicked the back of Daniil's neck with her stone-hard fingers. Petya said, "Look, this thing isn't getting any lighter."

"You sure you aren't here to collect anyone?" Daniil asked.

"As you can see, we've already collected. Now let us in."

Daniil stood aside and the men lumbered in with the coffin, trampling on shoes without taking off their own, scratching the wallpaper.

"Yasha, we'll have to move the cot to make room," Petya said.

"Which one?"

"Pink flower sheets."

"Keep holding your end while I set mine down," Yasha instructed. "Toasty in here, eh?"

"Yes, mind the heater by your feet," Daniil chimed in.

"I'll have to step out on the balcony while you pivot."

Baba Ola lunged at the men, yelling something about the balcony, but no one understood exactly what.

A panicked brood of hens stormed the room.

Aunt Nika clutched at her chest. "Sweet Saint Nicholas."

"We'll have to report this poultry enterprise, Citizens," said Petya.

Daniil was about to tell them these strange hens must have hopped over from another balcony when everything went dark.

The heater's rattle ceased. The hens were stunned silent. Through the window, Daniil could see that the neighboring buildings were blacked out as well.

"Electrical shortages," Yasha said. "Heard about it on the radio. Said to stay tuned for scheduled blackouts."

"Setting the coffin down," Petya said, voice strained. "It's about to slip out of my hands—"

"Slow, slow—"

A delicate, protracted crunch—the sound of slowly crushed tin—filled seventeen pairs of ears. Daniil had counted: seventeen, if you included the man in the coffin. For a few seconds, no one said a word.

"Well, looks like we're going to be here awhile." Yasha sighed and shuffled, and the stale smell of socks wafted through the air. "Wasn't there some jerky going around?"

Daniil's head whirled. Seventeen humans in one room, arms and legs and fingers and toes laced together. Plus one bay leaf. The crunch of the space heater replayed in his mind, even as the cold seeped in. A small clawed foot stepped on his. Seventeen olives. Daniil would die just like this, stuffed and brined with the others, their single coffin stuck in someone else's bedroom. No one drinks the brine anyway. A brush of feathers huddled on his feet, shivering. Daniil took a step forward, and the feathers swished past. In the dark he felt for the coffin, yanked out the crumpled space heater from underneath it. The corner of the coffin slammed against the floor. The children screamed.

Daniil stepped onto the balcony, flung the heater over the ledge. For a second he felt weightless, as if he himself had taken to the air. A hollow crash echoed against the walls of the adjacent buildings.

He stepped back inside and sank down on his bunk. Wood chips scratched between his fingers.

Grandfather Grishko was the first to speak. "Daniil, go down and get it." The whispered words were slow, grave. "We'll get it fixed."

What was his grandfather hoping for? Still, Daniil would

do as he was told, if only to get out of the crowded suite. Then he felt the cold steel of his uncle's mallet and chisel among the wood chips. He grabbed the instruments and descended to the ground floor. A gruff voice offered caramels but Daniil snatched the bencher's cigarette lighter instead. He lit its flame, illuminating the red stenciled numbers on the front of the building.

And then he knew what he had to do. He had to get heating, because heating meant Number 1933 Ivansk existed. And if the building existed, he and his family had a place, even in the form of a scribble buried deep in a directory. He would show them proof. He would show the ones behind the glass partitions—he would bring the stenciled numbers to them. Daniil positioned the chisel. The first hit formed a long crack in the concrete, but kept the numbers whole.

LITTLE RABBIT

Sometimes they arrive in vans from the maternity ward. Sometimes in strollers, or inside shawls wrapped around waists. Sometimes from the village, sometimes from the town. Few of the babies have names. If they arrive healthy, they were born unwanted; if wanted, then unhealthy.

The baby house sits tucked behind a hill, out of sight of the village and the town.

It's bad luck to talk about or show pictures of the babies living at the baby house, much like it's bad luck to talk about or show pictures of a train wreck or a natural disaster.

The main hall of the baby house has bright windows and three rows of beds, and a *sanitarka* who makes rounds with a milk bottle. She strokes the babies, talks to each in turn.

She says, "My kitten."

She says, "I wish I could keep you for myself."

She says, "They told your mother to try again."

The director of the baby house is young, eager, and progressive. He's the darling of the Ministry of Health. The beam of light piercing the fog. The broom battling the cobwebs. Within the first year of his tenure, he urged the Ministry to take a holistic approach to the issue of invalid care. Since adult invalids are classified as Group Ones, Twos, and Threes according to labor capacity, the director believes each baby's group number can be predicted—projected—at birth. That way the Ministry can anticipate the resources necessary for lifelong collective care.

According to the director's classification of infants, the Threes have a minor defect. It may be cosmetic—webbed fingers, a misshapen ear—but when has that helped a person land a job? Even the outwardly normal babies pose a risk. Abandonment is taxing, and there is always the chance of a depressive mother, an alcoholic father lurking in the genes. So the director deems the healthy but abandoned babies Threes, just in case.

Twos are blind and/or deaf. Skin disorders and ambiguous genitalia fit the criteria, too.

Ones simply lie there.

An aerial view of the baby beds looks like this:

[ ] [ ] [ ] [ ] [ ] [ ] [ ]
[ ] [ ] [ ] [ ] [ ] [ ] [ ]
[ ] [ ] [ ] [ ] [ ] [ ] [ ]

This year, the Ones, Twos, and Threes sleeping in their beds look like this:

[3] [3] [2] [3] [2] [3] [3]
[2] [1] [1] [1] [1] [1] [2]
[3] [2] [3] [3] [3] [2] [3]

The director would deny any pattern to the distribution of the babies. If the healthier babies lie next to the great bright windows where they can chatter with the magpies, and next to the doors where the occasional Ministry inspector can see them best, it's surely a coincidence. Pick any other room, where the older children sleep—though they rarely sleep, not all at once—and try to find a pattern in that jumble.

And anyway, it's the *sanitarki* who assign the babies to their beds, not he.

In this particular batch of babies, the loudest voice comes from row three, bed seven. The puzzle pieces of her face hadn't sealed together in her mother's womb. A cleft begins at her right nostril, plunges down the upper lip and into the hole of her mouth. A boisterous Three, just on the edge of invalidity, this girl is one of the favorites. She coos and babbles and peekaboos, flirts with the *sanitarki,* grips their fingers with an iron strength when they peer in at her.

At six to ten months, the babies begin to crawl. Hands and knees patter on the vinyl floors. Today the distribution of the crawling babies looks like this:

```
3   2   3   2 33
    3   2 3     3
3   2 2   3 2           3
```

On the far right, the lone baby: she's the lively Three. Faster than the others, the girl has slipped out of the baby house. She's cruising along the wooden picket fence, eyes set on a gap wide enough to squeeze through. Pine trees tower beyond it, beckon

her with their syrupy smell. Four pickets to go, three, two . . .
The same *sanitarka* who found the girl inside the medicine cabinet yesterday, an overturned dustbin the day before, catches up
to her now. As the girl sticks her head through the gap—the
air feels different on the other side, less dense—she feels her
romper tighten around her neck, pull her backward. The pines
slide away.

The *sanitarka* is doubled over, panting. "You'll be the end of
me." She lets go of the romper. The baby looks up at her and a
flutter of giggles escapes her mouth, wins her captor over like it
did yesterday and the day before.

A small, secret relief for the overworked attendants: not all
the babies learn to crawl. This failure is only natural for those
with clubfeet or spinal conditions. And if some of them aren't let
down from their beds, it's because they'll never be able to walk
anyway. Beds take up most of the space, and there aren't enough
sanitarki eyes to watch over everyone. If all the babies learned to
crawl, where would they go?

The older children name her Zaya. Little rabbit. Her mouth is a
crooked assemblage of teeth and gums. As the teeth grow, they
poke through the slit in her lip. At breakfast, half her porridge
oozes from her nose.

The name starts with a letter she can't pronounce, and the
other children delight in hearing her try. There are many letters
the girl can't pronounce, because they require both sets of lips
and a complete upper jaw.

Whenever a *sanitarka* goes for a smoke in the courtyard,
Zaya follows. Most of the time the woman sits in silence, staring at the wall opposite, taking grateful pulls on her cigarette.

On good days she reads a magazine; on the best days she reads aloud to Zaya, who learns to follow the words. Topics covered: newly released books, home remedies, the latest five-year economic plan, hat etiquette.

Every New Year's Eve, the baby house receives a donation from the Transport Workers' Union. A six-wheel truck sighs to a stop in front of the gates, enveloping the waiting children in a great diesel plume. Grandfather Frost—whom a recently orphaned boy calls "Saint Nicholas" before receiving prompt correction—descends from the passenger side. He wears a tall boyar hat, a long white beard, a blue velvet coat, and felt boots.

Grandfather Frost beams down at the children. "Who's been good this year?"

The children shrink back, alarmed by the question.

Grandfather Frost recoils, too, unaccustomed to children afraid of the prospect of gifts. He whistles up to the pock-faced man behind the wheel, who wears a plastic crown festooned with a shiny blond braid—Snow Maiden. The bed of the truck lifts, dumps a pile of old tires over the fence. Grandfather Frost uses shears to cut the tires into swans.

"It's a miracle," says a *sanitarka*, and so it is. The children keep silent, watch the miracle unfold. This is how Grandfather Frost does it:

1.

2.

3.

4.

Soon the courtyard is littered with dusty brown swans. The children paint the swans red or blue or yellow. At first Zaya mixes red and yellow in her tin to make a radiant orange, but an experimental dab of blue turns the mixture brown.

When the director of the baby house comes to Zaya's swan, he says, "That's a shame. Grandfather Frost gave you three bright colors to choose from."

Zaya invents an explanation, one the director would find very clever, and would surely repeat to his colleagues at the Ministry, who would find it very clever also—but of the sounds that slosh out of Zaya's mouth, the director understands none.

So he asks, "Why not just paint the swan yellow?"

Every spring, the *sanitarki* trim the hedges along the building, pull weeds around the tulips. They bleach and starch the curtains, pour ammonia over the floors, shine the doorknobs, wipe the babies down.

And every spring, the Psychological-Medical-Pedagogical Commission of the Ministry of Education arrives in a procession of three cars. Zaya and the other four-year-olds press themselves against the windows of the baby house, watching the procession in a quiet panic. They are about to be redistributed.

The Threes shouldn't worry. Unless they freeze up during the test, they'll move on to the children's house.

The Ones don't yet know they should worry. They can't even get out of their beds, and no one can do anything about that now, so they'll be transferred to the psychoneurological *internat*.

"What's at the *internat*?" asks a pudgy-cheeked boy, twice caught wearing a dress in the laundry room.

"It's a delightful place where children run barefoot, pick berries," says the director, who has popped in for the day. "Communicate with nature, and so on."

A *sanitarka* starts to weep.

"Happy tears," the director explains.

The Twos are the wild cards. Sometimes the Commission sends them to the children's house, sometimes to the *internat*.

Zaya, our solid Three just a few months back, has regressed to a Two. She has abandoned speech in favor of writing, but few of the children know how to read yet, so most of the time she points and grunts.

When it's Zaya's turn with the Commission, the director escorts her to the back of the building, to a small room that smells like moldy onions. The Commission members sit at the head of a long table. They've arranged themselves in descending order of height, like nesting dolls. The largest man, who has a thick mustache cascading from his nostrils, asks Zaya to confirm her name.

Zaya hopes this isn't part of the test, but knows she must answer every question, without exception. She fears that her bottom is about to give out like a trapdoor, jams her knees together, afraid of wetting herself. To deflect, Zaya does what she saw a *sanitarka* do once, with the director, to get an extra day off. She twists her finger in her curls, peeks at the men through her thick lashes. She leans in, coy, as if she wants to tell them a secret. The men lean in, too. First she raises three fingers, then seven. When no one says anything, Zaya forces out a giggle: Silly, can't you understand?

The largest man looks down at the file in front of him and laughs. "Row three, bed seven. Her sleeping assignment." This answer satisfies the Commission.

The man in the middle, with oily porous cheeks, pushes four puzzle pieces across the table. Zaya fits them together. It's a picture of a cat, dog, and parrot.

"Can you tell us what you see?"

Zaya stares at the cat, dog, and parrot. She feels the shape of the first word inside her mouth, whispers it into her hand. It doesn't come out right, so she moves on to the next word, then the next.

~~CAT~~
~~DOG~~
~~PARROT~~
~~BIRD~~
~~THING~~
~~WITH~~
~~FEATHERS~~
~~PETS~~
~~ZOO~~
~~ANIMALS~~
~~FLUFFY~~
~~FRIENDS~~

The Commission watches the clock above the girl's head. The inside of Zaya's palm is warm and wet from her breath. At last the smallest of the men says, "One more question and you're free to go. What's the weather like outside?"

Zaya swivels around, looks out the window. All she wants is to run out of the building, out to where the weather is. Instead, she turns back to the Commission, presses her hands to her ears to keep from hearing herself, starts pushing the first word out. Its mangled syllables resonate between her palms. She wishes the Commission wouldn't look at her. She shuts her eyes, bangs her fist against the table, louder, louder to keep from hearing herself, until the pressure in her chest breaks and the words fire out. "How bright and beautiful the sun," she cries, "not one cloud can cover it up!"

The psychoneurological *internat* stands at the edge of a cliff, overlooking the Dnieper River. Patches of white plaster flake off the walls to reveal pink brick underneath, as if the building suffers from a skin condition. Long ago, before its gold-plated cupolas were dismantled and its eighteen copper bells melted down to canteen pots, before its monks were shot, it was a monastery. An iron fence, a recent addition, surrounds the grounds, its spiked rods rising high enough to keep in the tallest of the children, the space between the rods narrow enough to keep in the smallest.

The fresh batch of five-year-olds arrives in the back of a decommissioned camo truck, hair and faces dusty from the road. A tall woman in a dark green suit—their new director— orders the children to gather round in the courtyard. Her large smooth forehead emits a plastic sheen. One hand rises in greeting as the other does a head count. The children who can stand prop up those who can't against the fence.

Zaya watches a group of teenagers blow dandelion fluff at each other in the distance, two of them barefoot, just as the previous director promised. She scans the courtyard for tire animals, sees in their stead fresh mounds of earth.

The woman points to a sheet-metal sign nailed to the arched entrance of the decommissioned monastery. "Can anyone tell me what that says?"

When no volunteers come forward, she reads the sign her-self: "THERE IS NO EASY WAY FROM THE EARTH TO THE STARS."

The reedy boy beside Zaya asks what stars are.

"To reach the stars you need to build a rocket. And we did that," the new director says. "But let me tell you a secret." She lowers her voice, and the circle of children tightens around her. "To build a rocket you need parts, and sometimes you get a crooked bolt, a leaky valve. These have to be thrown away. If they aren't, the rocket won't launch. Even if it does launch, it might explode into a million pieces."

The children nod along.

"That's just the way it is, when you're reaching for the stars." She casts a magnanimous gaze over the group. "Sometimes you get defective parts."

The children nod along.

"But we don't throw people away. We take care of them. You can bet on that for the rest of your life." She straightens up. "Something to think about, when you're feeling blue."

The children follow the director into the building. They file along a corridor, past the canteen; past a storage room con-taining a blackboard; past the latrine where a bald boy squats in the shadows, gargoyle-like, his shoulder blades jutting out; past a pair of twin girls balancing on one leg each; past a door with a tiny square window too high for Zaya to see through. They reach a cavernous hall crowded with beds and children. The painted walls are crowded, too, with scenes of wrath and deliverance: flames rise from the floor; a red snake coils up a wall and wraps its tongue around a thrashing figure; above are curly clouds, men with wings, men without wings, disembod-ied wings twisting around each other, stretching to the domed ceiling, at the center of which is a woman cradling a baby. The baby stares down at Zaya day and night wherever she is in the hall, its hand up, on the verge of uttering something important.

In the following months, Zaya adds to the pictures to pass the time. Using a sharp stone, she scratches the men's mouths open to let them speak. She wishes she could reach the never-sleeping baby, but it sits too high.

When winter comes, cold whistles through the cracks in the windows and into the lungs of the children.

It begins with a cough. The tickle in Zaya's throat burrows into her chest, blossoms into double pneumonia. She drifts in and out of a fevered fog. Noises filter into her dreams—the ruffle of sheets, snot bubbling up and down endless nasal passages, the distant cowbells from a village, the clack of trains from a rail yard.

Outside the window, a couple of older, healthier children chatter as they dig another pit. When she hears them shoveling earth back into the hole, Zaya feels for damp soil on her own hot face. But it isn't there; it's for someone else.

Green buds erupt on the branches outside. Sunrays on bed-sheets shine brighter.

When Zaya wakes between fevers, she sees a pair of with-ered arms and legs on her bed. She tries to move; the matchstick limbs answer. She covers them with her sheet.

Zaya looks at the beds around her. The room is hushed, so she's surprised to find most of her neighbors awake, blinking at the ceiling. She's in a different room than before, a white-tiled room—the room on the other side of the door with the tiny square window.

[1] [1] [1] [1] [1] [1] [1]
[1] [1] [1] [1] [1] [1] [1]
[1] [1] [1] [1] [1] [1] [1]

Zaya could try walking again, but where would she go? Everything aches, as if a fire has ravaged her insides. She lays her head down and goes back to sleep.

She wakes when a pair of fingers press on her wrist, checking for a pulse.

She wakes when the corners of her sheet lift and she floats in the air for an instant. She screams and falls back down on the mattress.

She wakes writhing in hot wet sheets. Something hard slams into her side. When she disentangles herself, she is on the floor. Her sweaty palms slip on pale pink vinyl as she crawls to the door with the square window. She tries the knob, beats her fists against the door. She slumps back down to the floor, a heap of bones. Coughs erupt through her mouth and nose in painful spasms, expelling a frothy pus—not into her hand, but in the crook of her elbow, as she has been taught. Two limp-faced girls gaze down at her from their own beds, peaceful. All she needs to do is let it happen, their heavy-lidded eyes tell her. Give in, melt into the floor. Isn't that what this room is for—a long rest? Her lungs will unclench, fill to the brim like two bottles of milk, and the *sanitarki* will take her away. That's when the parents come at last. Zaya has seen them visit once their child is safe in a small box. A nurse might even sew up her lip for the occasion.

Her head rolls to the right. In the corner of the room, a crack in the vinyl floor glows.

What she has to do is crawl toward that crack. The need is bodily, instinctual. She has seen it in every moth and mosquito bewitched by a flame.

Right hand, left knee, left hand, right knee. Her joints grind painfully, her elbows buckle, but she keeps moving.

Zaya lifts the corner of the vinyl. It peels away easily, revealing a pair of short loose planks. The glow beckons her from beneath them. Panting, she pulls the planks aside. A small hole in the floor opens up to a set of stone steps leading underground. The tunnel's cool breath gives the girl a burst of strength. She stands on shaky legs. Strings of cobweb cling to her arms and face as she follows the light down the cold steps, which level out into a chamber. Long narrow shelves are carved into the stone walls. Broken candles and vases litter the floor—remnants of pillage. The air smells sweet, like a baby's mouth after feeding.

The glow emanates from a corner of the chamber, from underneath a gray pile of robes. Zaya unwraps them—the cloth's folds retain a bluish luster—and the unsettled dust brings on another coughing fit. Inside is a mummified body. Or, half of one. The legs appear to have been snapped off. The brown leathery face squints up at Zaya. Its mouth, petrified midscream or midyawn, suggests the creature met its end in wretched terror or sublime repose. Its hair and beard are the yellow of dead grass, but its teeth gleam white. The hands cross at the chest, skin stretched between knuckles like a bat's wings. Beside the creature lies a dark red cylindrical hat Zaya has seen before, atop the bishops painted on the monastery walls—but on this hat, the jewels have been picked out.

Zaya beholds the shriveled face, and determines from its

gaze that something awaits her, something important. The saint, she knows, doesn't want to be buried at the *internat* any more than she does.

Zaya tugs the hat over its shiny forehead. The hat is fetching. A waste indeed, to be a saint stuck underground with such a hat.

She gathers the saint in her arms. Centuries of desiccation have made its body very light. The saint pulls forward, as though tied to a string. The pair make their way through the tunnels, turning right here, left there, the bundle leading her through the dark, urging her toward the miracle of escape. They totter up a set of steps, toward an opening. Zaya smells the leaves before she sees them. Gripping the saint with one hand, pulling the branches and weeds apart with the other, she climbs over a clutch of tree roots.

The blue sky greets them.

Zaya leaps forward, ready to run from the *internat*, run as far as her aching legs will take her. But then she stops.

They're outside the building, but still inside the tall iron fence.

Before Zaya can feel the blow of defeat, the bundle pulls her back into the tunnel—and Zaya follows.

Down the tunnel they go, then to the left, right, left again. They reach an opening in the cliff face. The only way down here is a fall to the jagged rocks below. Back into the tunnel they go. The saint's pull is stronger now, the pruney creature in Zaya's arms frantic to perform its marvel, and she frantic to witness it. Right, left, another left.

They're outside again, but still inside the fence, this time just a few steps shy of the forest beyond.

Zaya waits for direction. The saint, now inert, gives none. She shakes it. In the daylight, its parched features look exhausted, accepting their fate. At least one of them can escape, Zaya thinks. She thrusts the bundle over the fence. The saint lands faceup on the wild grass, hat uncapped in salute.

Zaya hears a *sanitarka* call her name, turns to see the woman racing toward her. Just a few meters away now, the woman's creamy arms are spread wide enough for an embrace.

When Zaya slides her leg between the rods of the fence, she doesn't expect the rest of her body to follow—but it squeezes right through. She picks up the saint, and runs for the pines.

LETTER OF APOLOGY

Don't think.
If you think, don't speak.
If you think and speak, don't write.
If you think, speak, and write, don't sign.
If you think, speak, write, and sign, don't be surprised.

News of Konstantyn Illych Boyko's transgression came to us by way of an anonymous note deposited in a suggestion box at the Kirovka Cultural Club. According to the note, after giving a poetry reading, Konstantyn Illych disseminated a political joke as he loosened his tie backstage. Following Directive No. 97 to Eliminate Dissemination of Untruths Among Party Cadres and the KGB, my superior could not repeat the joke, but assured me it was grave enough to warrant our attention.

One can only argue with an intellectual like Konstantyn Illych if one speaks to him on his level. I was among the few in the Kirovka branch of the agency with a higher education; the task of reeducating Konstantyn Illych thus fell to me.

Since Konstantyn Illych was a celebrated poet in Ukraine and the matter a sensitive one, I was to approach him in private rather than at his workplace, in case the joke had to be repeated.

Public rebuke would only be used if a civil one-on-one failed. According to Konstantyn Illych's personal file (aged forty-five, employed by the Cultural Club), the poet spent his Sundays alone or with his wife at their dacha in Uhly, a miserable swampland 30 kilometers south of town.

Judgment of the quality of the swampland is my own and was not indicated in the file.

The following Sunday I drove to Uhly, or as close as I could get to Uhly; after the spring snowmelt, the dachas were submerged by a meter of turbid water and people were moving between and around the dachas in rowboats.

I had not secured a rowboat for the task as the need for one was not mentioned in Konstantyn Illych's file, nor in the orders I was given.

I parked at the flood line, where five rowboats were moored: two green, two blue, one white, none black. Usually, our mode of transportation was black. I leaned on the warm hood of my car (black) and plucked clean a cattail as I deliberated what to do next. I decided on the innocuous white; I did not want to frighten Konstantyn Illych, and cause him to flee, by appearing in a black rowboat.

The dachas were poorly numbered and I had to ask for directions, which was not ideal. One man I spoke to was half-deaf and, after nodding through my question, launched into an account of his cystectomy; another elderly man, who clearly understood Russian, rudely responded in Ukrainian; one woman, after inquiring what in hell I was doing in her brother's rowboat, tried to set her Rottweiler on me (fortunately, the beast feared water). I was about to head back to the car when an aluminum kayak slid out of the reeds beside me, carrying two knobby-kneed girls. They told me to turn right at the electric transformer and row to the third house after the one crushed by a poplar.

A few minutes later I floated across the fence of a small dacha, toward a shack sagging on stilts. On the windowsill stood a rusted trophy of a fencer in fighting stance, and from its rapier hung a rag and sponge. When no response came from an oared knock on the door, I rowed to the back of the shack. There sat Konstantyn Illych and, presumably, his wife, Milena Markivna, both of them cross-legged atop a wooden table, playing cards. The tabletop rose just above water level, giving the impression that the couple was stranded on a raft at sea. The poet's arms and shoulders were small, like a boy's, but his head was disproportionately large, blockish. I found it difficult to imagine the head strapped into a fencing mask, but that is beside the point.

"Konstantyn Illych?" I called out.

The poet kept his eyes on the fan of cards in his hands. "Who's asking?"

I rowed closer. The wood of my boat tapped the wood of the table. "My name is Mikhail Ivanovich. Pleased to meet you."

Konstantyn Illych did not return my politesse, did not even take the toothpick out of his mouth to say, "You here for electric? We paid up last week."

His wife placed a four of spades on the table. Her thick dark hair hung over her face.

I told Konstantyn Illych who I was and that the agency had received reports of how he had publicly disseminated wrongful evaluations of the leaders of the Communist Party and Soviet society at large, and that I was here to have a conversation with him. Konstantyn Illych set his cards facedown on the table and said in a level tone, "All right, let's have a conversation."

I had conducted dozens of these conversations before and

always began from a friendly place, as if we were two regular people—pals, even—just chatting.

"Quite the flood," I remarked.

"Yes," confirmed Konstantyn Illych, "the flood."

"I'll bet the children love it here."

"No children."

Usually there were children. I stretched my legs out in the rowboat, which upset its balance, and jerked them back.

"No parents, grandparents, aunts, or uncles either," said Milena Markivna. Her upper lip curled—the beginning of a sneer, as if to say, But you already knew that, didn't you?

There had indeed been mention in the file of a mass reprimand of Milena Markivna's relatives in the fifties, but amid all the other facts about all the other residents of Kirovka, with all their sordid family histories, the detail had slipped my mind. Still, did the woman need to dampen the spirit of the conversation?

Konstantyn Illych broke the silence. "So what's the joke?"

"I hadn't made a joke," I said.

"No, the joke I supposedly told about the Party."

Already he was incriminating himself. "The term I used was 'wrongful evaluation,' but thank you for specifying the offense, Konstantyn Illych."

"You're welcome," he said, unexpectedly. "What was it?"

"I cannot repeat the joke." I admit I had searched Konstantyn Illych's file for it, but one of the typists had already redacted the words.

"You can't repeat the joke you're accusing me of telling?"

"Correct." Then, before I could stop myself: "Perhaps you could repeat the joke, and I'll confirm whether or not it's the one."

Konstantyn Illych narrowed his eyes, but said nothing.

"We aren't moving any closer to a solution, Konstantyn Illych."

"Tell me the problem first," he said.

A brown leaf, curled into the shape of a robed figurine, floated by Milena Markivna's foot. She pressed the leaf into the murky water with her thumb before turning to her husband. "Just say sorry and be done with it."

I thanked her for her intuition—an apology was precisely what was in order, in the form of a letter within thirty days. Milena Markivna advised me not to thank her since she hadn't done anything to help me; in fact, she hated officers like me and it was because of officers like me that she had grown up alone in this world, but at least she had nothing to lose and could do anything she wanted to: she could spit in my face if she wanted to. This, I did not recommend.

Konstantyn Illych was tapping his fingernails on the table. "I'm not putting anything in writing."

It is usually at this point in the conversation, when the written word comes up, that the perpetrator becomes most uncomfortable, begins to wriggle. Few people grasp the simple logic of the situation: once a transgression occurs and a case file opens, the case file triggers a response—in this case, a letter of apology. One document exposes the problem, the second resolves it. One cannot function without the other, just as a bolt cannot function without a nut and a nut cannot function without a bolt. And so I told Konstantyn Illych, "I'm afraid you don't have a choice."

He reached for the small rectangular bulge in his breast pocket. "Ever read my poetry?"

I expected him to retrieve a booklet of poems and to read from it. Dread came over me; I had never been one to understand verse. Fortunately he produced a packet of cigarettes instead.

"Come to my next reading," he said. "You'll see I'm as ideologically pure as a newborn. Then we'll talk about the letter."

Normally I had a letter of apology written and signed well under the thirty-day deadline. I took pride in my celerity. Even the most stubborn perpetrators succumbed when threatened with loss of employment or arrest. The latter, however, was a last resort. The goal these days was to reeducate without arrest because the Party was magnanimous and forgiving; furthermore, prisons could no longer accommodate every citizen who uttered a joke.

In Konstantyn Illych's case, next came gentle intimidation. If Konstantyn Illych stood in line for sausage, I stood five spots behind him. If Konstantyn Illych took a rest on a park bench, I sat three benches over. He pretended not to see me, but I knew he did: He walked too fast, tripping on uneven pavement; bills and coins slipped from his fingers regularly. His head jerked right and left to make sure he never found himself alone on the street. He needn't have worried—there was always the odd pedestrian around—and anyway, I did not intend to physically harm or abduct Konstantyn Illych, though that would have been simpler for both of us. My older colleagues often lamented the loss of simpler times.

Four days passed without a word exchanged between us.

On the fifth day, I attended Konstantyn Illych's poetry reading at the Kirovka Cultural Club. I took a seat in the front row of the lectorium, so close to the stage I could see the poet's toes agitate inside his leather shoes. In the dim light, I was able to transcribe some of his poetry:

> Helical gears, cluster gears, rack gears,
> bevel and miter gears, worm gears, spur gears,
> ratchet and pawl gears, internal spur gears,
> grind my body
> meat grinder
> grinds
> gr gr grrr
> ah ah ah
> aah aah aah
> ah haaaaaah!

And also:

> The bear
> bares his flesh
> skinless, bears the burden
> of the air wooooooooooooooosh

And also:

> Dewy forget-me-not
> not me forgets.
> Stomp.

I cannot guarantee I transcribed the onomatopoeic bits with accuracy; Konstantyn Illych's reading gave no indication of the number of *a*'s and *o*'s, et cetera.

At the end of the reading the poet placed his pages at his feet, unbuttoned his faded blue blazer, addressed the audience: "Time for some trivia. I'll recite a poem and one of you will guess who wrote it. Get it right and everyone here will admire you, get it wrong and you'll be eternally shamed." A few people laughed.

Throughout the challenge poets such as Tsvetaeva, Inber, Mayakovsky, Shevchenko (this one I knew), and Tushnova were identified. The audience expressed their enjoyment of correct answers by whooping and clapping between names.

Konstantyn Illych waited for the lectorium to quiet down before he leaned into the microphone. "Who, whom."

This, apparently, was also a poem; the crowd erupted in fervid applause. I made a mental note to alert my superiors that local culture was going down the chute.

Konstantyn Illych scanned the audience until his eyes met mine. "The gentleman in the front row, in the black peacoat," he said. "Who wrote that poem?"

Once more the hall fell silent.

I turned right and left, hoping to find another man wearing a black peacoat in my vicinity. That's when I saw Konstantyn Illych's wife sitting behind me. She crossed her arms, her great bulging eyes on me, beckoning me to answer. One of her hands, nestled in the crook of her opposite arm, resembled a pale spider waiting to pounce.

Konstantyn Illych's voice boomed above me. "The greatest poet of all time, Comrade, and you do not know? I'll give you three seconds. Three . . ."

I froze in my seat. The middle-aged man to my right, whose nose looked like it had been smashed many times, nudged me in the ribs.

"Two . . ."

The man whispered "Grandfather Lenin!"—a mockery that I found in poor taste.

"One!" Konstantyn Illych bellowed. "Who was it, esteemed audience?"

The words rose from the crowd in a column. "Grandfather Lenin!"

Konstantyn Illych looked down at me from the stage, tsked into the microphone. Each tsk felt sharp, hot, a lash on my skin.

It was around this time I began to suspect that, while I had been following Konstantyn Illych, his wife had been following me. I forced myself to recollect the preceding week. Milena Markivna never figured in the center of my memories—the bull's-eye had always, of course, been Konstantyn Illych—but I did find her in the cloudy periphery, sometimes even in the vacuous space between memories. If I stood five spots behind Konstantyn Illych in line for sausage, the hooded figure four spots behind me possessed Milena's tall narrow-shouldered frame; if I sat three benches away from Konstantyn Illych, the woman two benches over had the same pale ankle peeking out from under the skirt. I began to see my task of retrieving the letter of apology in a new light.

What I suspected: My mission was not about the letter, but about the lengths I would go to retrieve it.

What I suspected: I was being vetted for a position of great honor.

What I knew: "Who, whom" had been a simple test, and I had failed it.

What I knew: My mother had been subjected to the same tests as a young woman, and had succeeded.

When I was a child, my mother was invited to join the

Honor Guard. According to my father, she had always been a model student, the fiercest marcher in the Pioneers, the loudest voice in the parades. She was the champion archer of Ukraine and had even been awarded a red ribbon by the Kirovka Botanist Club for her Cactaceae collection. One evening, an officer came to our door and served my mother a letter summoning her to the Chief Officer's quarters. Within six months she was sent to Moscow for special training, as only special training would suffice for the Guard that stands at the mausoleum of Lenin. Since our family was not a recognized unit—my parents hadn't married because my paternal grandparents (now deceased) didn't like my mother—my father and I could not join her in Moscow. I was too young to remember much about this period, but do have two recollections: one, I could not reconcile the immense honor of the Invitation with the grief that plagued the family; two, my father assumed care of my mother's cactus collection, and every evening, when he thought I was asleep on the sofa bed beside him, wrapped his fingers around the spines of the plants and winced and grit his teeth but kept them there until his whole body eased into a queer smile. For many months his hands were scabbed and swollen. Within a year my father was gone also; he had at last been able to join my mother in Moscow. My grandparents told me that one day I, too, would join them.

Now that Milena Markivna had entered my life, I felt I had finally been noticed. The vetting process for the Honor Guard was still possible. My reassignment to Moscow to see my mother and father was still possible. I believed it was possible to make gains with hard work.

From that point on I followed Milena Markivna's husband with greater vigilance, and in turn Milena Markivna followed me with greater vigilance. If Konstantyn Illych rifled his pockets for a missing kopek for the newspaper, Milena Markivna's voice behind me would say, "Surely you have an extra kopek for the man," and surely enough, I would. If I dropped a sunflower-seed shell on the floor while pacing the corridor outside the couple's apartment, behind the peephole of Suite 76 Milena Markivna's voice would say, "It's in the corner behind you," and surely enough, it was. She was a master observer, better than I.

(It should not go unsaid that, beyond mention of the reprimand of Milena Markivna's family, and of her employment as a polyclinic custodian, her file contained little information. On the surface, this was because she was born in the province surrounding Kirovka and not in the town itself, but I suspected it was a matter of rank: if Milena Markivna were indeed my superior, tasked with the evaluation of my conduct and aptitude for ceremonial duty, of course I would not have access to her full history. Information is compartmentalized to mitigate leaks, much like compartments are sealed off in ships to prevent sinking.)

Konstantyn Illych grew accustomed to my omnipresence, even seemed to warm to it. Once, after a bulk shipment to the Gastronom, I watched him haul home a 30-kilogram sack of sugar. By the time he reached his building, Number 1933 Ivansk (at least, this was the theoretical address indicated in his case file—the building number appeared to have been chiseled out of the concrete), the sack developed a small tear. Konstantyn Illych would be unable to haul the sack up to the tenth floor without losing a fair share of granules. The elevator was out of the question due to the rolling blackouts, and so I offered to pinch the tear as he carried the load over his shoulder, and he did not decline. Many minutes later we stood in front of Suite 76, Konstantyn Illych breathless from the effort. Since I was there I might as well come in, he said, to help with the sack.

He unlocked the steel outer door and the red upholstered inner door, then locked the doors behind us—all this with an excessive jingling of numerous keys. Here was a man with a double door, he wanted me to take note: a Man of Importance.

The apartment was very small, surely smaller than the sanitary standard of 9 square meters allotted per person, and only marginally heated. After we maneuvered the sack to the balcony, I scanned the suite for a trace of Milena Markivna—a blouse thrown over a chair, the scent of an open jar of hand cream, perhaps—but saw only books upon books, bursting from shelves and boxes lining the already narrow corridor, books propping up the lame leg of an armchair, books stacked as a table for a lamp under which more books were read, books even in the bathroom, all of them poetry or on poetry, all presumably Konstantyn Illych's. A corner of the main room had been spared for a glass buffet of fencing trophies and foils, and on top of the buffet stood a row of family portraits. I tried to find Milena Markivna in the sun-bleached photographs but these, too, belonged to Konstantyn Illych—the large head made him recognizable at any age. I wondered if she lived there, if she was even his wife.

Milena Markivna entered the apartment a few minutes later, with a soft scratch of keys. After shrugging off her long black raincoat to reveal the bleach-flecked smock underneath—a marvelous imitation of a custodial uniform—she appraised me as I imagined she might appraise a rug her husband had fished out of a dumpster. Would the piece be useful, or would it collect dust and get in the way? Her expression suggested the latter, but her husband was leading me into the kitchen, the point of no return. Once a guest steps into the kitchen, to let them leave without being fed and beveraged is of course unconscionable.

Milena Markivna leaned her hip against the counter, watching Konstantyn Illych mete out home brew into three cloudy shot glasses. "Lena, fetch the sprats, will you?"

Milena Markivna indicated she needed the stool, which I immediately vacated. She stepped up on it to retrieve a can from the back of the uppermost cupboard, then set the can down on the table, with some force, and looked at me, also with some force, presumably daring me to do something about the unopened sprats. I produced the eight-layer pocketknife I always kept on my person. In an elaborate display of resourcefulness, I flicked through the screwdriver, ruler, fish scaler and hook disgorger, scissors, pharmaceutical spatula, magnifying lens, hoof cleaner, shackle opener, and wood saw, before reaching the can opener. Its metal claw sank into the tin with so little resistance, I could have been cutting margarine. Milena Markivna must have noticed the surprise on my face. She asked if I knew about the exploding cans.

I conceded I did not.

"It's something I heard," she said, "something about the tin, how they don't make it like they used to. People are getting shrapnel wounds." After a pause, she gave a dry mirthless laugh and so I laughed as well.

Before Konstantyn Illych passed around the shots, I laid a sprat on my tongue and chewed it slowly to let the bitter oil coat the inside of my mouth and throat, minimizing the effects of the not-yet-ingested alcohol.

I took note that Milena Markivna also chewed a sprat before the first shot.

Three rounds later, Konstantyn Illych was speaking of the tenets of futurist philosophy. He was about to show how he employed them in his poetry when I jumped in to ask about the letter of apology, due in fifteen days.

"Mikhail Ivanovich," he said. "Misha. Can I call you Misha?"

"You may." The home brew was softening my judgment and there was only one sprat left.

"Fuck the letter, Misha. What is this, grade school?"

I told him about the possible repercussions, that he might be fired or arrested. "You're lucky," I said. "In earlier times, a political joke meant ten years."

Konstantyn Illych set his empty shot glass upside down on his index finger like a thimble, twirled it in languid circles. "Once upon a time," he began.

I wanted to shake the letter out of him.

"I got the flu," he continued. "Ever get the flu?"

"Sure."

"The flu turned into bronchitis and I ended up in the hospital. Not only did I get my own room, but by the end of the week the room was filled, and I mean floor-to-ceiling filled, with flowers and cards and jars of food from people I didn't even know, people from all around the country."

Milena Markivna placed the last sprat between her lips and sucked it in until the tip of the tail disappeared into her mouth.

Konstantyn Illych leaned in. "Imagine, Misha, what would happen if you tried to get me fired."

Another week passed without success. My superior remarked that I was usually quicker at obtaining a letter, and was I not dealing with someone who specialized in the written word, who could whip up a heartfelt apology in no time? I considered bribing the poet, but the mere thought felt unnatural, against the grain, against the direction a bribe usually slid. I began to neglect other tasks at work but still believed my persistence with Konstantyn Illych would be rewarded. I admit I thought of Milena Markivna as well, and often. She followed me into my dreams. Throughout my life, she would tell me in those dreams, I had been watched over. She would award me with a certificate signaling my entry into the Honor Guard, would place on my head a special canvas cap with a golden star on its front. I cannot say if this image is true to the initiation ceremony, but it was how I imagined it had happened with my mother. I would wake at night to find myself alone in my dark room but felt no fear. I knew I was being watched over.

The day before the deadline I stood at the back of the town cinema, watching Konstantyn Illych watch *Hedgehog in the Fog*. Eventually my attention turned to the animated film itself. I had already seen it a number of times and always found it unsettling—similar to the way heights are unsettling. En route to visit his friend for tea, Hedgehog gets lost in the fog that descends on the forest. It isn't the fog or the forest that troubles me, although they trouble Hedgehog; what troubles me is this: Hedgehog sees a white horse and wonders if it would drown if it fell asleep in the fog. I've never understood the question. I suppose what Hedgehog means is: If the white horse stops moving, we would no longer see it in the white fog. But if we no longer see it, what is its state? Drowned or not? Dead or alive? The question is whether Hedgehog would prefer to keep the fog or have it lift only to discover what is behind its thick veil. I would keep the fog. For instance, I cannot know the whereabouts of my parents because they are part of me and therefore part of my personal file and naturally no one can see their own file, just like no one can see the back of their own head. My mother is standing proud among the Honor Guard. My mother is standing elsewhere. She is sitting. She is lying down. She is cleaning an aquarium while riding an elevator. Uncertainty contains an infinite number of certainties. My mother is in all these states at once, and nothing stops me from choosing one. Many people claim they like certainty, but I do not believe this is true—it is uncertainty that gives freedom of mind. And so, while I longed to be reassigned to Moscow and look for my parents, the thought of it shook me to the bones with terror.

When the film ended, I felt a damp breath on the back of my neck. Milena Markivna's voice whispered: "Meet me at the dacha at midnight. I'll get you the letter."

It was a weekday, a Wednesday, and so the dachas were empty of people. The swamps were still flooded, but this time a sleek black rowboat waited for me. It barely made a seam in the water as I rowed. Northward, the overcast sky glowed from the lights of the town. My teeth chattered from cold or excitement or fear—it is difficult to keep still when one knows one's life is about to change. Already I could feel, like a comforting hand on my shoulder, the double gold aiguillette worn by the Guard. The tall chrome leather boots tight around my calves.

I tried to retrace the route I had taken the first time I visited the dacha, but found myself in the middle of a thicket of cattails. The glow of the sky suddenly switched off. (Normally electricity is cut not at night but in the evening, when people use it most, and thus the most can be economized—this is the thought I would have had had I not been engulfed in panic.) Darkness closed in on me. I circled on the spot. The cattails hissed against the edge of the boat. Willow branches snared my arms and face. A sulfurous stench stirred up from the boggy water. Milena Markivna had given me the simplest of tasks and I was about to fail her.

A horizontal slit of light appeared in the distance, faint and quivering. I lurched the boat toward it. Soon I recognized the silhouette of the shack on stilts, the light emanating from under its door. I scrambled up the stairs, knocked. The lock clicked and I waited for the door to open, and when it did not, I opened it myself.

A figure in a white uniform and mask stood before me, pointing a gleaming rapier at my chest. The figure looked like a human-size replica of the fencing trophies I had seen inside the glass display in Suite 76.

"Close the door." The voice behind the mask was calm, level, and belonged to Milena Markivna.

I tried to keep calm as well, but my hand shook when it reached for the handle. I closed the door without turning away from her, keeping my eyes on the rapier. The ornate, patinated silver of its hilt suggested the weapon had been unearthed from another century.

"Down on the floor. On your knees."

I had not imagined our meeting would be like this, but did as I was told. I inquired about the utility of having my ankles bound by rope and Milena Markivna explained it was to prevent me from running away before she was done. I assured her I wouldn't think to run from such an important occasion and she, in turn, assured me she would skewer my heart onto one of my floating ribs if I tried. Before she stuffed a rag inside my mouth, I told her I had been waiting for this moment since I was a child, and she replied that she had been waiting for it since she was a child as well. I told her I was ready.

She said, "I'm ready, too."

I do not know how much time passed with me kneeling, head bowed, as Milena Markivna stood over me.

I tried to utter a word of encouragement, perhaps even mention my admiration for the canvas cap with the golden star on its front, but of course I couldn't speak through the rag in my mouth. All I could do was breathe in the pickled smell of the fabric.

She knelt down in front of me, one hand on the hilt of the rapier, its tip still quivering at my chest. With the other hand she took off her mask. Hair clung to her forehead, moist with sweat. I searched her face for approval or disappointment but it was closed to me, as if she were wearing a mask under the one she had just removed. I wondered how this would all look if a stranger barged through the door: she almost mad and I almost murdered.

At last Milena Markivna stabbed the rapier into the floor, which made me cry out, and said there was really no hurry. She brought over a stout candle that had been burning on the table and dipped my fingers into the liquid wax, one by one, as she named her relatives who had been executed, one by one, thirty years ago. The burning was sharp at first—although I dared not cry out or make another sound—but soon felt like ice. Milena seemed calmer after this. She removed the rag from my mouth, unlaced her boots, set her bare feet on top of them, and gave me a series of instructions. As I bowed my head and enveloped her warm toes in my mouth—they had a fermented taste, not unpleasant, like rising dough—she reminded me how she hated me. I removed my lips from the mound of her ankle long enough to tell her that we were not so different, she and I; that I, too, had grown up alone, even though my solitude would end soon. As she picked up a second candle and began to tip it over my scalp, she asked how it would end. Barely able to speak now, I told her that it would end when she inducted me into the Honor Guard and I would go to Moscow and see my family again. She laughed as if I had told a joke. My head pulsed with pain; tears blurred my vision. The smell that greeted me was of singed pig flesh, sickening when I realized it was my own. Milena Markivna set the candle down and asked how I knew of my family's whereabouts. I said it was what I had been told. As she slid her fingers along the blade of the rapier, she said the neighbor who had taken her in had promised that her family had gone to a better place, too, but never specified where or explained why they never wrote. The darkness of the night filtered in through the cracks of the shack and into my mind, and I began thinking of things I did not like to think about—of my mother and father and where they really might be. Milena Markivna wrapped her hand around the hilt of the rapier again and told me to take off my coat and shirt and lie facedown on the floor.

As I did so, one thought knocked against the next, like dominoes:

There was a possibility I was not, at present, being recruited.

If not, there was no Honor Guard waiting for me.

If not, my parents' rank did not matter.

If not, my parents did not have rank.

If not, Mother was not in the Guard.

If not, they were not in Moscow.

The blade dragged from my tailbone up the thin skin of my spine, searing my mind clean. I screamed into my mouth so that no one would hear. When the blade reached between my shoulders it became warm, and from its point a sweet numbness spread through my arms. I thought of my father with his bleeding hands, understood that queer smile. My head spun and the walls began to undulate. My voice came hoarsely. "How do you know what happened to your family?"

After a moment she said, "They disappeared. That's how I know."

"They could be anywhere."

"Do you believe that?"

"Yes." My body shook against the damp floorboards. "No."

It was when I welcomed the blade that it lifted from my skin. I felt a tug between my ankles, then a loosening. She had cut the rope.

"You can go."

"You're not done."

"No," she said, but still she pushed my shirt and coat toward me with her foot. I lay limp, spent. Through the window I could see the glow of the town flicker back on. I remembered why I had come to the dacha, but could not rouse myself to bring up the letter. I found I did not care about it much myself. I would be the one who would have to issue an apology to my superior tomorrow, giving an explanation for failing to complete my task. I would write it. My superior would read it. I would be dismissed. What next? I would stop by a news kiosk on my way home, search my pockets for the correct change. If I did not have it, a voice behind me might ask if someone has a kopek for the man. Surely enough, someone would.

Before leaving, I asked Milena Markivna, "What was the joke your husband told?"

"Oh." She said, "███████████████████████████████ ██████████? ████████████████████████████████."

"All this trouble for that?"

It was the first time I saw her smile. "I know. It's not even funny."

BONE MUSIC

The first time Smena's neighbor knocked on her door, she asked to borrow cloves. The woman stood in Smena's doorway, clutching a canvas sack to her chest. Her diminutive frame barely reached the latch. "I'll bring the cloves back," she promised. "You can reuse them up to three times."

This neighbor, Smena knew, associated with the building's benchers. The woman never sat with them but did spend a good deal of time standing beside them, cracking sunflower seeds, no doubt gossiping, and Smena would often hear the metallic clang of her laughter through the bedroom window. Smena had placed the woman in her mid-sixties, around Smena's age, but up close her wet lips and bright caramel eyes made her look younger. Her cropped hair, dyed bright red, reminded Smena of the state-made cherry jam she used to see in stores.

She did not let the neighbor in, but made sure to leave a crack between the door and its frame so as not to shut it in the woman's face—word got around if you were rude, especially to a bencher or bencher affiliate. Smena rummaged in her kitchen drawers for the cloves, then continued the search in her bathroom cabinet, which contained the kitchen overflow. There, the cloves rattled inside a newspaper pouch; they'd lost their peppery tang.

Smena stepped out of the bathroom and blurted "Oi." The neighbor was sitting in her kitchen. The woman had taken off her clogs, and a grayish middle toe poked through a hole in one of her socks.

Neighbors rarely visited each other, and if they did, it was to complain about a leak in the ceiling or to spy out who had better wallpaper and why. Smena tossed the pouch of cloves on the table, hoping the woman would take what she'd come for and leave.

"I'm Nika, from fifth," the neighbor said. "Have a biscuit." From her canvas sack she produced a small plastic bag, rolled down its rim, and Smena felt a pang of delight: inside were the same cheap biscuits Smena used to buy at the bazaar, the ones that had the shape and consistency of a fifty-kopek coin and had to be soaked in tea to save teeth from breaking. This gesture meant her guest wanted tea, which she, the host, should have offered long ago, upon greeting.

Nika craned her neck for a better view down the corridor. "Say, this a one-room or two-room?" Nika pronounced her words with a dawdling slur that was at odds with her quick movements. Smena wondered if the woman was recovering from a stroke.

"Two-room."

"For one person?"

Smena tensed. Anything she said, already she could hear being repeated around the block. "My husband snored." This was true: Smena had shared the sofa bed with her daughter, in the other room, until the girl had moved in with her fiancé's family many towns away.

To occupy herself, Smena set the kettle on the stove. When she turned back to the woman, beside the biscuits lay a black plastic sheet. An X-ray scan. Smena recognized it instantly; she had a stack of them in the cupboard beside the refrigerator.

"I hear you make a nice ruble copying vinyl records onto X-rays," said Nika.

Smena's brows lifted in mock surprise. "Who told you that?"

"A friendly worm in the ground."

"The friendly worm is mistaken."

"I used to own a few bone albums myself, a long time ago," Nika went on. "Only played them a couple times before they got worn through. Didn't compare to vinyl, of course, but that's how you got the real music." By "real" she meant banned music. American rock 'n' roll, decadent capitalist filth, the stuff with sex and narcotics. Smena's specialty. She had begun copying bootlegged albums in the postwar years, when she and her husband were desperate for money and radiographic film was the cheapest, most readily accessible form of plastic. Now, with the national shortage of reel cassettes—the national shortage of everything—Smena was back in business.

"I hear your records are the best," said Nika. "Can play for days."

Smena hunched her shoulders in an attempt to make her broad frame appear small, innocuous. "I don't know what you're talking about. I'm a simple pensioner, just like you."

"A simple pensioner like me doesn't have a two-room all to herself."

Smena detected judgment in Nika's voice—it was uncouth for a woman, especially one far along in her years, to take up so much space—but also envy.

When the kettle whistle blew, Smena was wary of turning her back to the woman again; she imagined discovering a pile of X-rays, or the woman's entire family, in the kitchen. She reached a hand behind her hips to turn off the gas, fumbled with the cutlery drawer for a spoon—then stopped. This was the same drawer that contained the lathe for engraving X-rays. Smena used her fingers to pinch tea leaves into cups, and stirred the tea by whirling each cup in a circle.

"I hope you can help me," said Nika.

"Sugar in your tea?"

"Please. Say, ever got an X-ray done yourself?"

"Everyone has."

"The radiation alone is enough to kill you, just slower than whatever it is they're checking for." Nika paused, as though waiting for Smena to say something. "What were they checking for?"

"A bout of pneumonia, a couple years ago," said Smena, distracted. She'd remembered the sugar jar lived in the same cupboard as the record player—which was a perfectly mundane object in itself, but not if seen in conjunction with the lathe. "I forgot, I'm out of sugar."

The two women drank their tea bitter. Smena observed that once, when Nika made to dip her biscuit, she missed the cup, tapped the table instead, noticed the error, and dipped the biscuit into her cup with vigor. Before her guest left, Smena tried to push the X-ray back into her hands, but Nika refused. "I'll be back with your cloves," she said from the doorway.

"Keep them."

"You can reuse them up to three times. I read about it."

"Keep reusing them, then."

"Oh, I couldn't."

Smena forced a smile. "It's a gift."

"I'm the one who should be gifting you gifts, for helping me."

"I haven't done anything to help you."

"But you will," said Nika. "I can always pick out the good people. Like good watermelons." She was about to head off at last, then paused and turned to face Smena again. "You said your husband snored. What fixed it?"

"He died."

Nika winked. "I'm divorced, too. They say our building is cursed."

Smena closed the door on the woman, to hide her own blush. She shoved the X-ray in the garbage bin under the sink. Her underground business made Smena vulnerable to extortion. If Nika visited again, she might ask for more than cloves.

But the X-ray did not stay in the bin long.

Smena's worst traits, her mother had once informed her, were her height and her curiosity.

It was the golden hour, the best time of day to inspect new X-rays, when sunbeams shot directly through Smena's kitchen window, illuminating each feathery detail of the bones. Smena lived on the tenth floor, and the neighboring building was far enough from hers for the X-ray viewings to be conducted in privacy. She secured Nika's scan onto her window with suction cups.

The profile of a skull shone at her. The architecture of a human head never failed to shock Smena, or make her wonder how such a large bulbous weight balanced on the thin stack of vertebrae.

Smena couldn't help but feel excitement: a head X-ray did not come her way as often as those of other body parts. And heads were the most popular with the buyers, fetched the most money. A shame she couldn't use this one. She would not be lured into Nika's trap.

The small white letters on the bottom right-hand corner of the film, easily overlooked by the untrained eye, read VERONIKA L. GUPKA, TUMOR. Smena noticed a thinning at the base of the skull, a shadow overtaking it from inside. The thing looked contagious, like a curse. She didn't like the tumor hanging on her window, projecting its tendrils onto her kitchen wall.

She understood then: the woman was dying. Whatever she wanted from Smena stemmed from this fact.

Smena hid the scan, but this time, despite herself, she did not try to dispose of it.

Megadeth's growls and screams, banned in all fifteen Soviet republics, came from Smena's cupboard record player—at minimal volume, of course.

"I'm with the Kremlin on this one," said Milena, Smena's dealer. "If these are the latest tunes from the West, maybe the place really is rotting." As usual, Milena stood leaning against the windowsill, ignoring the vacant stool in front of her. She seemed to prefer heights, like a cat, Smena had noticed.

This was their biweekly meeting. Milena brought wads of cash from selling bone albums at subway stations, public squares, and parks, and Smena counted the profit, taking the largest cut for herself. Next, Milena presented her with an array of X-ray scans procured through her job as a polyclinic custodian, and Smena picked out the most desirable designs. Today's winning selection included a foot that had been subjected to an asphalt roller; a handsome pelvic girdle; a torso with what looked like a prominent colon but was really the spine of a fetus; a child's hand curled into an obscene gesture.

Smena had recruited Milena because of her proximity to X-rays, but also for her proximity to Smena herself. Milena lived two doors down in a one-room she shared with her poet husband, and Smena didn't even need to cross her own doorway to coax her neighbor in for a chat. From the first, Smena had known Milena would be perfect for the position; no one would suspect the pale middle-aged woman with drab clothes and uneven bangs of dealing illicit albums. At first Milena had refused, recounting how just last month she'd had to shake off a government lackey who had been trailing her husband, and was not sure she would be able to get rid of another, but after a second round of shots Milena confessed she could use the extra money. She was saving up—what for, she didn't say.

Seated across the kitchen table from Smena was Larissa, the style hunter who supplied hits from the West. "Megadeth is a deliberate misspelling of the English word 'megadeath,' one million deaths by nuclear explosion," she explained. Unlike Milena, who wore only black like a perpetual mourner, Larissa was a carefully choreographed explosion of color: red-and-yellow checkered dress, tangerine tights, peacock-blue heels (which she hadn't taken off at the door). She sewed most of her clothes herself, copying styles from British and French magazines, complete with embroidered duplicates of the most prestigious logos. Thirty-one years old, Larissa lived with her mother and two daughters in the suite below Smena's. From the fights Smena overheard through the heating vent—typical topics raised by the mother: Larissa's low-paying job at the chemical plant two towns over, Larissa's expensive tastes, Larissa's failure to keep a man—Smena had gauged that her downstairs neighbor, like Milena, could not refuse a second income. It had only taken

Smena two nights of thumping her floor with a broom handle before an irate Larissa paid her first visit.

Smena closed her eyes, taking in Megadeth's restless rhythms. She couldn't understand the lyrics, of course, but the singers' screams were so wrenching, they seemed to be dredging up bits of Smena's own soul. She wondered how Megadeth would sound at full volume, the power of the screams unharnessed.

"I think there's something to this," she said.

Milena's and Larissa's eyes swiveled to her in surprise.

Smena glared at the women in return. "Oh, come off it. I'm old but I'm not obsolete."

"The group's aesthetic is contextual. People scream a lot in America," offered Larissa, adjusting her horn-rimmed lensless glasses. "They have screaming therapy for terminal patients. Very expensive. I read about it. Doctors drop patients off in the middle of the woods and get them to hurl their lungs out. Barbaric, yes, but most come back happier."

"The last time I made a person scream they didn't seem any happier," Milena remarked with a smirk, "and I did it for free." Smena nodded without comment, assuming Milena was referring to one of her fencing tournaments.

When the meeting ended and Milena left, Smena found herself alone with Larissa as she gathered her effects into a quilted faux-leather purse. Smena leaned across the table toward the woman and stretched her lips over her teeth into a smile. This felt awkward, so she unstretched them. "You're doing a fine job, Larissa."

Larissa simply nodded, without deflecting the compliment. Another of her imports from the West: a lack of modesty.

Smena produced two bills from her pocket. She did not look

at the money as she slipped it into Larissa's breast pocket. She wanted the action of touching money to look easy, as if it was something she did a lot, something she barely noticed anymore. "I hear the bakery by the chemical plant is better than the one around the block. Mind picking up a loaf sometime this week?" she said. And added, "Keep the change."

A child's whining cry reached them from the suite below. Larissa gave a weary smile. "I'd be happy to."

"And a dozen eggs, if you see them."

"At the bakery?"

Smena slid a few more bills across the table, many more than necessary.

"Brown or white?" asked Larissa.

"White bread, brown eggs." The pricier options.

Smena had asked Milena to bring potatoes two weeks prior. If Milena and Larissa picked up an item or two of food for her every now and then, with her small appetite she would be fine. She did not want her neighbors to suspect that, combined, they were part of a greater pattern. She hadn't been to the bazaar in over a year, hadn't even ventured past her front door. Each time Smena opened the door, she felt the dank air of the outer hallway cling to her skin, as if she were being pulled into a tomb.

Smena's fears had begun with a newspaper article: a boy had tripped over exposed rebar and broken both wrists. For years, the townspeople had been privately griping about the poor state of roads, sidewalks, bridges, but this was the first time the consequences of decaying infrastructure were publicized. Soon more and more reports came, from all over the country, each more outlandish than the next. A sinkhole trapped a commuter bus. A family of five plummeted to their deaths in an elevator malfunction. A gas leak gently poisoned preschoolers for weeks before being discovered. Pedestrians were advised to avoid underpasses.

Even previously privileged information was released, about how the town had been built on a not-quite-drained marsh that was slowly reliquifying. Smena's daughter, and her daughter's university friends, had cheered on the liberation of the press, which was taking place in their respective towns, too. But Smena had felt safer under the maternal hand of censorship.

Smena's building, her entire town, now felt like a death trap, but she convinced herself that the concrete walls of her own apartment were secure. After a yearlong renovation, none of the windows or doors creaked. The new checkerboard linoleum felt smooth and sturdy under her feet. As long as she stayed in her space, twelve by twelve steps, she would be safe.

The X-ray of Nika's skull lay on the kitchen table. Smena admired its smooth round shape. No matter how penetrating the radiology waves, the thoughts and desires within that doomed chamber remained secret. There Nika lived, and there she would die.

Smena felt no pity. Pity masked itself as kindness, but was rooted in condescension. Smena would not want to be pitied herself.

She turned Megadeth back on. Screaming therapy, she thought. Now there's something useful.

She lit a cigarette, and paused to appreciate the scratchy vocals and pulse-raising tempo before hitting Stop, resetting the needle to the beginning. Using manicure scissors, Smena cut the radiograph into a circular shape. She made a hole in the middle of the circle with her lit cigarette, right where the ear would be, and the acrid smell of burning plastic rose from the film. She positioned the film on the phonograph, attached a spidery metal arm from the record player's needle to the cutting stylus on the phonograph, and hit Play on both machines. As the grooves on the vinyl vibrated the needle and produced music, the metal arm transmitted the vibrations to the cutting stylus and reproduced the grooves onto Nika's skull.

The evening before the next meeting, Larissa's eleven-year-old daughter knocked on Smena's door. Given Larissa's talent for fashioning replicas, Smena found it fitting that Dasha should look just like her wide-eyed mother—down to the cowlick, and the platoon of bobby pins enlisted to flatten it. The girl informed Smena that her mother couldn't make it to their biweekly study session on dialectical materialism—Smena couldn't help smiling—because her mother was so sick with the flu she couldn't crawl up two flights of stairs to tell Smena Timofeevna so herself.

Smena dropped her smile, remembering. "Eggs? Bread?"

Dasha tilted her head, confused. "No thank you." She turned on her heel and skipped down the corridor, purple dress rustling.

Smena spent the next hour scouring her kitchen, making a mental inventory of the remaining food: three potatoes, two bread heels, nine walnuts, one thimble-size jar of horseradish. Her millet and rice stocks had run out the month prior. If she cut down her already meager consumption, she estimated the supplies would last less than a week.

The smell of boiling chicken now wafting from the heating vent did not help calm Smena's nerves.

One thing Smena would not do was call her own daughter. After the grandchildren started coming, occasionally the daughter called to suggest Smena come live with her and her family in Crimea. They could sleep on the sofa bed together like old times, her daughter would joke, figure out a cot for the son-in-law. Smena would hear the shrieks of the grandchildren at the other end of the line and try to imagine herself as the babushka depicted in children's folktales: stout, puffy-cheeked, bending over a cauldron of bubbling pea soup with a wooden spoon in hand, ready to feed, bathe, rear an entire village.

"The time isn't right for a move," she had told her daughter the last time they spoke. "I'm too busy."

"Busy with what?" Her daughter didn't know about the bone business. "You're all alone over there!"

Smena took this to mean, "You're going to die alone over there," which was where the conversation always headed, and promptly hung up.

Smena's mother had birthed six other children before she had Smena, and had made a point of telling her that a husband and children were the best insurance against dying alone. The family had lived in a crumbling clay house. One day, when Smena's father was at work and she and her siblings were at school, Smena's mother took her metal shears and slashed away at the tall grass outside the window. The blades crunched into an electric cable. Smena was the one who found her mother's body in the weeds. Smena remembered how her own throat had contracted in shock, how her scream had come out as a hiccup. For a long time Smena had studied her mother's face, which was set in a wild openmouthed grin, as if she were biting into the sweetest happiness on Earth. Seven children, eighteen years of cleaning, chiding, spanking, loving, pea soup making, and what did it matter? Smena's mother had died alone, and seemed to have fared all right. Before the accident, Smena had imagined death as a send-off, a majestic ship to board while your party of relatives crowds at the port ledge, waving goodbye. The higher the attendance, the more valued your life. Now, she imagined something more private. Once you got past the ugly physicality of death, you were left with a single boat, a cushion. Room to stretch out the legs.

The second time Nika knocked on the door, she returned the cloves in their newspaper pouch. From the doorway she beamed up at Smena, as though she had proven herself by fulfilling her ridiculous promise. She produced a baking tray of buns from her cloth sack. Fragrant, buttery, they bulged out of the tray in a tight grid, ready to spring into Smena's mouth. Each had a neat hole on top, from a clove.

"Borrower's interest," Nika joked. Her speech had slowed since the last visit, her syllables become more labored.

Smena didn't know whether it was the hunger, or the shock at this small act of kindness—albeit suspect kindness—that made her say, "Come in for some tea?" before she could stop herself.

"Oh no, thank you. I couldn't." But already Nika was kicking off her clogs. "Just for a minute." She was wearing the same faded socks, with her toe sticking out. Smena offered a pair of furry dalmatian-print slippers, ones Milena usually wore during their meetings.

As Smena brewed tea, Nika separated the buns and arranged them in a circle on a glass platter—also conjured from the magical sack. "Got any butter?" She was quick, antlike, and before Smena could intervene, she opened the refrigerator. The expanse of white gaped at her, empty. With horror Smena imagined this detail registering in the neatly categorized inventory of Nika's mind, and wanted to snatch it back out.

Without comment Nika turned and marched out of the apartment, leaving Smena to wonder if the state of the refrigerator had offended her. But a few minutes later Nika returned bearing not only butter, but also bread, eggs, and a pat of lard wrapped in a plastic bag, for frying. She began piling the supplies into the refrigerator.

"You don't have to do that," said Smena. "I was going to go to the Gastronom tomorrow."

"So was I. We'll go together?"

Smena pretended to consider it. "Actually, tomorrow's no good."

"The day after."

"I'm tied up."

Nika shut the refrigerator, gave its handle a conciliatory stroke. "The benchers told me they haven't seen you leave the building in months," she said softly. "They only see your visitors, not you."

Blasted benchers, Smena thought. Nothing better to do. "Most of those old stumps are half-blind," she said. "And I move very fast." She pulled a bill from a metal tin on the counter, knowing she risked insulting the woman. But Nika only laughed, swatted the money away. "Please," she said. "*Kak auknetsja, tak i otkliknetsja.*" Do as you would be done by.

The women sat down together. Smena's discomfort melted away when she took her first bite of bun. Its thin caramelized crust, where egg whites had been painted on in crisscross, protected a warm flaky interior. The best bun she had ever tasted.

Nika ran her hand along the chrome length of the table. "This is nice. Quiet. Where I live it's a zoo. Fourteen people, another one in my daughter-in-law's belly. Imagine! Despite his position, my son and his family still haven't been assigned their own peace."

Smena wondered if she meant "place," and if the tumor was pressing a fibrous finger on just the wrong spot. "Which factory does he work for?"

"Timko works for the government." She let the last word fall heavily, significant.

Perhaps this was a threat? Working for the government meant anything from licking envelopes to spying on high-profile citizens.

"A nice two-room, is that so much to ask?"

Smena wasn't sure to whom, exactly, the woman was directing the question. But there it was: the dying woman's motive. A lovely two-room for her lovely family. Her legacy secured. If Smena were to be imprisoned for the bone business, Nika's growing, government-affiliated family would be next in line for her apartment. Smena wanted to jump up, scream "Gotcha!" like she'd seen a man do at the bazaar once, after he'd stabbed his finger into a vendor's pot of golden honey to reveal the cheap sugar syrup underneath.

Before Nika left, she placed a second sheet of black film on the table, without inquiring about the first.

An hour later, the new scan glowed on the kitchen window. Smena wanted to track the progression—again, for curiosity's sake.

The sun's rays showed more thinning of the bone as the

tumor burrowed toward the spinal column. Smena couldn't help being impressed by the thing—an organism living by its own will, clawing for space in the tight dome of the skull.

The next meeting, Larissa forgot about the bread and eggs, but did bring two albums by John Coltrane.

"Never heard of him," said Milena, who stood at the window, left thigh resting on the sill.

Larissa straightened the velvet lapels of her blazer and looked up at Milena. "John Coltrane," she explained, "was one of the most prominent jazz musicians of the twentieth century." Her nose and cheeks were red and puffy. Despite her best efforts to appear composed, she looked in danger of crumpling to the floor any moment.

"How am I supposed to know? No one's ever asked for a Coltrane," said Milena. She eyed the tray of buns poking over the top of the refrigerator, then glanced at Smena for permission. Smena nodded—she regretted not having offered them herself.

"You're supposed to *know* what you're selling," said Larissa, hoarse voice rising. Smena shushed her. "How else do you test for fake clients, impostors?" Larissa whispered.

"Speaking of," Milena said through a mouthful of bun.

Smena and Larissa turned to her.

"It's probably nothing," Milena tried.

"Tell us the nothing," said Smena.

Milena scratched a spot of grime off the window with her fingernail. "I was at the park, my usual spot by the thousand-year oak, when a guy came up to me. Skinny, with a sad attempt at a mustache. Asked for a KISS. Like the group. The music group."

"Very good," said Larissa, rolling her eyes.

"I started to grill him," Milena continued. "Year the band got together, band leader's middle name, year of their breakout single, whichever useless facts Larissa shoves down my ear." She winked at Larissa, who turned away in a huff. "The guy was doing well, seemed to know everything. Then he started grilling *me*. Asked why Ace Frehley added eyeliner to his iconic 'Space Ace' makeup design. What was I supposed to do, look stupid? I played along, answered best I could, but when I asked, 'So are you buying the album or not?' he only said, 'Nah, I got what I came for.'"

"And then?" asked Smena.

"He just walked off."

Milena helped herself to another bun. She mashed the entire thing into her mouth, and Smena watched her masticate it without any apparent enjoyment. There were only four buns left, and she imagined what would happen once they were all gone, how she'd gnaw on laurel leaves, suck peppercorns for taste.

After a while Milena said in a low voice, "It's what *they* do. Play with you first, see you flail, knowing you have nowhere to go."

"Play is all it is," countered Larissa. "No one gets sent to the camps anymore. Human rights," she proclaimed, chin tilted up, "are in vogue."

"My sweet thing," cried Milena. She sank down to the stool beside Larissa, grasped the young woman's hand. At first Smena took Milena's outburst for sarcasm, but Milena seemed genuinely shocked by Larissa's innocence, as if she'd discovered a kitten playing in a dumpster. Larissa blushed, but did not retract her hand before Milena let go.

When Smena had starting making bone records, in the fifties, the risks were clear, the boundaries stable. Now an invisible hand was loosening the screws, but it was impossible to tell which screws, and for how long the loosening would last. Although no one got sent to the camps (for now), every citizen was able to imagine more clearly than ever before what might await them in those very camps; the newspapers had begun publishing prisoners' accounts, down to the gauge of the torture instruments.

"Camps or no camps," Milena said, "prison wouldn't be fun either." She turned to Smena. "So what do we do?"

"You didn't show the man any of the albums?" Smena asked. "You kept them inside your coat the whole time?"

Milena nodded. "He saw nothing."

While the possible punishment was unclear, something else was not: they all needed the money.

Larissa turned to Milena. "When the man asked why Ace started using eyeliner, what did you say?"

"To keep the silver face paint out of his eyes. He's become allergic."

Larissa smiled proudly.

Now Nika visited Smena every week. She would bring soup or cabbage pie, and the pair would sit down for a midday meal followed by tea. Each time Nika knocked, Smena vowed to confront her. If Nika really was looking to extort her, Smena was willing to preempt, negotiate, even give her a cut of the bone music profits. But confronting Nika would also mean admitting to the business, and what if the woman wasn't willing to negotiate? And, a distant possibility: What if Nika wasn't trying to extort her at all? More and more, Smena was willing to believe it.

In truth, she didn't mind Nika's visits. The woman's chatter offered a lens into the outer world that the newspapers—which Smena had mostly stopped reading anyway—could not. From Nika, Smena learned that the irises were blooming, the flowers floppy as used handkerchiefs; that it was the time of year when woodpeckers drummed on utility poles down by the river, to woo their mates. Nika exclaimed, "Can you imagine the ruckus?" Yes, Smena could.

Week to week, Smena watched the change in Nika over the rim of her teacup. One visit, Nika's slur was so pronounced Smena could barely understand her, and the pair sat in silence, pretending nothing was wrong. Another visit, Nika regaled Smena with jokes, but as she spoke her face lacked expression, as though she were posing for a government identification photo.

"You keep giving me a funny look," Nika remarked on that occasion.

Smena tried to brush it off. "I'm impressed. You tell a joke but keep such a straight face."

"I'm losing feeling in my face."

"Oi."

"My daughter-in-law says it'll do wonders for the wrinkles."

"The brat."

"I'll look all the better when they bury me." A strand of hair fell over Nika's eyes and her hand pecked at her forehead, trying and failing to find the strand.

"You should be in the hospital, Nika."

The women locked eyes.

"So you've looked at the scans," said Nika.

"I don't know why you keep giving them to me."

Nika shrugged. "They're as useless to me as they are to the doctors who order them."

"What do you mean?"

"The polyclinic has quotas for tests, so they do tests. Or they just make the numbers up to fill the quotas, so their money and supplies don't get cut. The polyclinic's filled with these ghost patients and can't admit new ones."

"You have a growth in your brain the size of a lemon and they can't admit you?"

"They can't admit me *because* of the lemon. I'm not a viable patient."

"With your new face I can't tell when you're joking."

"Really, Smena, when was the last time you went out into the world?" Nika sighed, as if she were about to explain basic arithmetic. "The polyclinic doesn't want to exceed their death quota."

"Which I'm sure they've made up."

"Doesn't matter. The nurse said if they exceed the quota, they get investigated, and if they get investigated, it's worse for all of us."

"How nice of her to give you an explanation."

"It was," she said softly. "I gave her chocolates."

Smena looked at her neighbor. She was a shell of the woman who had first come to Smena's door two months ago, determined to get her way.

"At least you can make something useful out of the scans," said Nika. "Something beautiful."

Smena heaved herself to her feet. A vertiginous feeling overwhelmed her. She saw herself on the edge of a precipice, its bottom beckoning. She feared heights, perhaps because she also loved them—she always wondered what would happen if she jumped.

Smena swung open the cabinet above the fridge. She

retrieved the five albums she had made for Nika and spread them out on the table in chronological order. She pointed to the first, the Megadeth. "You won't like this one at first but it'll grow on you. Listen to it when you're alone, and imagine the sounds pouring from your own mouth." She pointed to the rest: "Pink Floyd, to relax to. Suzi Quatro and Julio Iglesias, to cheer up to." Nika studied the scans on the table, the ripening shadow at the base of the cranium.

Smena set the fifth, Coltrane, on the record player, and watched Nika see her skull spin into a milky blur as the needle sucked music from the grooves. The horn section came in, ecstatic, then melted away into the oily tones of solo sax. Nika closed her eyes, swayed lightly to the music. At the end of the song Smena lifted the needle from the record. She searched her friend's face for a twitch, a nudge, but was met with an unsettling blankness.

Nika opened her eyes. "Thank you."

Smena gathered up the bone albums. "Take them, they're yours."

"I said you were a good watermelon. Didn't even have to thump you to know it. Didn't I tell you?" Nika took the scans, placed them in her cloth sack with great care.

Smena wasn't sure what to say, or why she settled on "Cut me up and eat me."

"Don't think I won't."

"I'm all seed."

"I'm smiling, Smena. You just can't tell."

When Nika made to leave shortly afterward, Smena asked, "No more scans for me this week?"

Nika shook her head. "No more."

—

A few days later, Smena woke to hurried knocking on her door. On the other side of the peephole: Milena. Smena checked herself in the hallway mirror, discerned the blurry shape of her body through her thin cotton nightgown. She swung a fur coat over her shoulders before unhinging the locks.

"Heading out?" Milena asked when she stepped inside.

"Yes," Smena lied. "You'd better make this quick."

Milena locked the dead bolt behind her. "I got approached again," she said, her posture unusually straight. "Not by the same guy as last time, but this one was just as wormy. He gave me a record." From her long raincoat Milena produced a yellow vinyl sleeve, the same type Smena used for distribution. She slid out a bone album, set it on the record player. Smena recognized the perky melody. The Beach Boys. The quality of the copy was poor, mostly scratching and bubbling, as though the singers were being drowned.

After a few seconds, the music cut out.

A man's voice came on, in low and booming Russian. *Came for the latest tunes? You're done listening.* A slew of curses dipped in and out of the hisses and pops.

Smena let out a bark of nervous laughter. "Hardly the latest tune. That song is almost twenty years old."

"Smena Timofeevna." Milena hadn't used Smena's patronymic in years, and the sudden formality was more frightening than the cursing still blasting from the player. Milena slowed the record to a stop with her thumb. "We're fucked."

She looked at Smena, expecting instruction.

Smena picked up the X-ray record and did what she did with every new X-ray that fell into her hands: she hung it on her kitchen window. The morning light shone strong enough for her to make out a pair of lungs and a shadow of a heart. The center hole of the record had been burned through the aorta. With a sickening familiarity, she saw the tiny bulbous alveoli filled with mucus, laced around the bottom of the right lung. Pneumonia. Right where her own had been, a couple years ago. Since the corners of the film had been cut off, she couldn't check for the patient's name. Many people get pneumonia, she thought. This could be anyone's scan. Still, she couldn't shake the suspicion it was hers. It made her uneasy, to think of looking at her insides outside her own body, as though she were being dissected. She felt a peculiar wringing in her chest, a hand palpating her organs. She thought about the few people in her life who knew she'd been sick: her daughter. And, most recently, Nika.

Since Nika's first visit, Smena had known that she'd been caught. But she'd been foolish enough to believe the woman wouldn't follow through with her scheme. She'd allowed herself to forget: neighbors never visited each other.

She curled her fingers into fists, uncurled them, let her hands flop to her sides. "We'll need to warn Larissa."

"I just did. She almost seemed happy about it, our little martyr. Made me promise to teach her sparring techniques." Milena saw the pained look on Smena's face. "Don't worry about her. She comes from a model family with a squeaky-clean record. Worry about yourself."

Smena walked around the room, aimless. She took vinyl albums from the bookshelf at random, put them back. With Larissa's careful hands, each original sleeve and center label had been replaced with state-approved ones, from acts like Jolly Fellows, Good Guys, Contemporanul, Red Poppies. That Smena's music library presented as perfectly flavorless had always amused the three women, an inside joke. Perhaps she could keep just one or two albums? She briefly let herself entertain the possibility, then admonished herself. If back in the fifties keeping one album would have been as risky as keeping one hundred, why should things be different now? She turned to Milena, who was stationed by the balcony door, watching in silence. "We'll need to get rid of the equipment," Smena said. "And the music."

Milena gave a curt nod. "Leave it to me, Smena Timofeevna."

From her wardrobe Smena retrieved a linen sheet. She wrapped it around the record player and phonograph. "Wouldn't want them to get scratched." With utmost care she placed the cutting lathe and its metal arm into a pillowcase. She slipped the forbidden vinyls into another, trying not to think of the effort Larissa had put into procuring them. It would only take Milena two trips to her husband's beat-up Kombi, parked in the courtyard, to make the bone music studio disappear.

When Milena came up to get the second load, Smena asked, "What will you do with yourself now?"

"Leave town, get lost in the countryside. Something I've been saving up for anyway." Milena was trying to sound casual, but Smena thought she detected a tremor in her voice.

"Hard to imagine your husband in the country." The last time Smena had seen him two balconies over, polishing a loafer, she'd marveled at his delicate hands.

"Isn't it." Milena shot Smena a sly look, and for one moment Smena thought she intended to leave him behind.

Milena stalked down the hall with the rest of the equipment, her footsteps eerily quiet. Smena wondered if she would ever see her neighbor again. Then she imagined leaving her own apartment, sharing a sofa bed with her daughter again, and her daughter's husband, and her daughter's husband's family, and all those lovely, spirited grandchildren, and the knobby cats they brought home from the streets. She wept into the sleeve of her fur coat.

Smena was searching her apartment for tools or X-rays she might have overlooked when she heard the wail of a siren. She dropped to the floor. Her heart flapped against the linoleum, loose and arrhythmic. She wanted to shush it so the downstairs neighbors wouldn't hear. The siren grew louder, until it reached their building, then cut out. Hurried footsteps echoed from the depths of the building, but never reached her floor. Smena crawled to her bedroom window, peeked out. The source of the siren was not the police but an ambulance. After a few minutes, a pair of paramedics emerged from the building's entryway carrying a stretcher, and on the stretcher lay Nika. Sunlight glimmered on her cherry-red hair as the paramedics loaded her into the ambulance. Smena wanted to rush downstairs and—what? Strangle the woman? Embrace her? Both?

The vehicle lurched into motion, rounded the street corner, and disappeared.

Smena stood back from the window. She was still wearing the fur coat. The coat would have to do. The polyclinic was only four blocks away, but she thought she might be away for longer than the four blocks and so made preparations. She retrieved her reserve of cash from a jar hidden in the toilet tank, packed a few changes of clothing into a duffel bag. A dull ache set into her knees and hips from the earlier drop to the floor, from the crawling, but she quickened her movements, ignoring the pain.

Smena swung her door open, and stepped over the threshold. The exterior corridor was cold, dimly lit, smelled of stale tobacco. The damp climbed her calves and thighs, made her shiver in her coat. She wanted to turn around, banish the hostile world with a flick of the dead bolt. But her apartment had lost the protection it once held.

Taking the elevator was out of the question. Clutching the rickety metal banister, Smena descended one step at a time. She tried not to look at the cracks in the walls. A piece of candy perched on a stair and she reached for it before thinking, hungry, but the puffy wrapper was hollow inside, a child's trick. The entranceway at the ground floor greeted her with the stench of garbage and urine, a waft of boiled potatoes.

Smena stepped outside and, for the first time in more than a year, felt live air move across her face. Her windows and glassed-in balcony had been sealed against drafts—she'd forgotten that drafts could feel nice, like a gentle tickling. She parted her lips, let the warm autumn light fill the cavity of her mouth and throat.

"I'll be damned! She's alive," exclaimed one of the pensioners on the bench outside. The man had acquired a new sprinkling of moles and sun spots on his face since the last time she'd seen him. "How long's it been, Smena Timofeevna?"

"Too long, Palashkin," she answered.

She shuffled on, her feet unsteady on the cracked slabs of the sidewalk. The concrete ten-stories around her were identical to the one she had just exited, and Smena had the impression she was walking the same block over and over. She kept her eyes on the ground. She stepped on a curled dry leaf and its crunch underfoot delighted her. She stepped on another, then another, progressing leaf to leaf. Parts of the roads sagged. The edge of the town, where the sunflowers normally grew, was being closed in by cattails. Let it all sink, she thought. She imagined herself and the townspeople on the bottom of a great marsh, to be discovered centuries later, open-eyed, their skin blue, hair orange from the gases, preserved for eternity.

The next time she looked up, she stood in front of the building she thought might be the polyclinic. The gleaming white-tiled edifice in her memory cowered under the poplars, its walls matte with graffiti, many of the tiles missing.

Inside, wooden benches lined the walls of a small lobby. A nurse pushed a mop around the floor, transferring dirty water from one corner of the room to another. It didn't take long to find Nika, who lay on a wheeled bed in a corridor off the lobby. The two paramedics who had collected her were arguing with the receptionist. As Smena approached Nika, the expression on her neighbor's face transformed from happy surprise to terror. By the time Smena reached her bed, Nika had lifted the covers over her nose, as though expecting to be hit.

Smena stepped back. She'd been feared before, certainly—by Milena and Larissa, whenever she chastised them for an oversight—but not like this. It stung. "You can move your face again," she observed, attempting a level tone.

"Now it's my feet."

"Where's your son and the rest of them?"

"Work, the park, and the belly," said Nika. "But you came." It sounded like a question, Nika wondering aloud which version of Smena had come: the vengeful or the forgiving one. Smena still wasn't sure herself.

"So they're finally admitting you," said Smena.

Nika nodded at the men and receptionist yelling at each

other. "To be decided." She lowered the cover from her face. The skull with which Smena had become so well acquainted shone under Nika's pale, cracked skin, its outline disturbingly visible, now in three dimensions.

Nika gave a nervous laugh. "This is a bed, Smena. Look at it. It doesn't fold into anything. It's not a couch or a desk or a storage box. It's a bed and you don't feel bad lying in it. Try it."

"What?"

"This bed. You're going to try this bed." Nika pushed her head and shoulders into her pillow, wriggled the rest of her body toward the rail at the edge of the bed. Smena thought Nika was playing a joke until a pale leg poked out from under the sheets and draped itself over the rail.

"No, Nika—" She grabbed Nika's bony ankle. Nika swung a second leg over the rail, and now Smena held on to both ankles. "Keep down, will you?"

"You can't know till you're in it."

Nika's breaths were heavy, rasping, and Smena now saw the immense strength Nika's seemingly whimsical gesture had required. She heaved Nika's legs back onto the bed, rearranged the sheets.

"Tell you what," said Smena. "When you're well again and ready to go home, we'll get you a real bed. A big one. Have your son and his family move into my apartment. I don't need the space anymore. And as for me, if you want, I mean, only if the prospect doesn't sound too awful—"

"You'll move in with me." Nika's face softened. "It'll be like back in the dorms," she said. "But only the best parts. No exams. And you'll take the bed. I'll take the foldout."

"We'll get two beds. They'll take up the whole room."

"What if one of us takes a lover?"

"We'll work out a visitation schedule."

Nika looked up at the ceiling, spread her arms and legs out, letting herself float in the daydream. "If only we'd decided all this sooner."

"It's not too late." It felt so easy now, to play along, to plot their future together. Smena stroked her friend's hair. The roots were oily and she longed to grab them by the fistful, let the musky sheen settle between her fingers.

The nurse with the mop was eyeing them. Smena said, "I have to go." Where, she wasn't sure. It would be midday, the sun at its warmest. She could go to the bazaar, buy something to eat right from the stalls. Fried dumplings, filled with mushrooms or ground beef. Or sour cream, fatty yellow and runny, which she'd drink straight from the jar. And afterward? She could go anywhere, board any bus or train. The thought was terrifying and thrilling.

"Wait till I'm asleep," said Nika.

Smena didn't have to wait long.

MISS USSR

On Monday morning, the phone on Konstantyn Illych's desk rang. He reached for the receiver without taking his eyes off the budget sheets spread before him.

"You didn't alert us to the beauty pageant," said a woman on the other end of the line. She introduced herself as Irina Glebovna, the new Minister of Culture—his most superior superior. Never before had a Minister called the lowly Kirovka Cultural Club. He turned down the steady prattle of the radio, welcoming the interruption.

"My sincerest apologies," he offered. "Did you want to enroll?"

She ignored this. "Contestants lined up around the block. A victory parade. A marching band, Konstantyn Illych? With what funds?" She drew out her vowels but swallowed the word endings, exaggerating a posh Muscovite accent.

"People volunteered. Civic duty."

"I heard a recording of the winner's talent routine." She was referring to Orynko Bondar's singing of "The Glory and the Freedom of Ukraine Has Not Yet Perished," once the anthem of Ukraine, banned by Moscow since 1922. "The singing," Irina Glebovna remarked, "it wasn't very good."

Konstantyn did not disagree. He hoped this was all the Minister had to say on the subject.

"I can't help but think"—here her voice sharpened, a butter knife swapped for a boning knife—"that the girl, your Miss Kirovka, earned her title on political grounds."

Aesthetic grounds, Konstantyn wanted to argue. Orynko possessed an outlandish beauty: moonlit teeth, freakishly large amber eyes, long silvery hair that doused her back and shoulders like mercury. But Konstantyn, being what he was—a slouchy forty-seven-year-old male with an uncertain marital status—thought better than to extol a teenager's looks. He settled on "The judges chose her, not I."

"You must be pleased with yourself." The Minister's tone suggested the opposite. "Your counterpart in Kiev was so charmed by your contest, she was about to organize one at the national level—Miss Ukraine SSR."

"Whatever Kiev is planning, I have nothing to do with it." Yet Konstantyn couldn't help chuckling, proud his pageant idea had caught on.

"Kiev is no longer planning," the Minister corrected. "But next thing we know, it'll be Miss Estonia SSR. Miss Latvia SSR. Miss Georgia SSR. Miss Chechen-Ingush ASSR." Konstantyn knew that each of the countries she listed had been the site of recent mass demonstrations, calling for independence.

"And so? You can't stop them all." He regretted the words as soon as they tumbled from his mouth, knowing he'd gone too far.

After an awful pause, the Minister's words were soft, measured: "You'll make an announcement revoking the girl's title."

Konstantyn waited, hoping the Minister would break into laughter. This was the sort of thing the preceding Minister of

Culture was rumored to have done: pretend to bestow punishment, then tease his victim for being so easily duped.

"I understand it's a difficult time." The Minister's speech had regained its false drawl. "When was it your wife left you? Three months ago?"

Three months and six days; how did the Minister know? Konstantyn had come home from work to discover the Kombi gone, along with Milena's fencing gear and a few items of clothing. Milena's departure had left him spinning like a leaf blown from its branch; he stopped writing, relegated himself to mundane administrative tasks. Their marriage had never been passionate, but he'd envisioned her always being there, stoic and dependable, like a grandfather clock. Whenever he fell ill, she'd leave a pot of broth on the stove before work, and whatever it lacked in taste it made up for in nutrition. When he wrote a new poem, she was the first to hear him recite it, dutifully setting her book on her lap, even though her eyes might not have left its pages.

"At least, no children to split," the Minister kept on, in studied sympathy. "No need to prove yourself to anyone, Konstantyn Illych. I'll have a journalist give you a call. One small correction and you're done."

When the phone rang again an hour later—likely the journalist—Konstantyn did not pick up. He would wait this one out. Surely the press and the Minister had more important matters to attend to, and would soon forget about his dethroning statement, his backwater town.

Konstantyn had reverse-engineered the Miss Kirovka pageant from its American equivalent. He'd heard the broadcast of

Miss America 1989 on Radio Liberty that autumn, dubbed in Russian. It was the applause that caught his ear: the thunderous volume suggested an audience numbering hundreds, even thousands. All the while his Club's attendance had been dwindling for years, along with state funding. There was a time when the lectorium would fill for history talks and poetry readings; now the one meager draw of the Kirovka Cultural Club was Viktorina, an arcade game that tested a player's ability to identify traffic warning signs.

On a sheet of graph paper, Konstantyn had taken note of the Miss America pageant's key parts: the talent round, the bathing suit round, the gown round. He'd jotted down bits of contestants' speeches, observing how each sentence inflected upward, toward a bright future. Konstantyn had inferred, from the exclamations of the judges, the geometry of contestants' bathing suits. As he'd listened, he couldn't help imagining one of those Yankee county fairs he'd read about, with their livestock breed shows, but pushed this thought from his mind. He hadn't cared for the banter of the host, who seemed to forget that this was above all a competition, but such details could be tweaked. What was important was the applause. And the admission fee.

As it turned out, Konstantyn was among the many Kirovkavites who had tuned in to Miss America. What was American was countercultural, which made it trendy: Levi's and Coca-Cola had found their way into Soviet homes; the opening of a McDonald's in Moscow was less than a year away. So it was that Kirovkavites met the news of their very own pageant with a cautious, tight-lipped excitement. On the morning of the event, contestants of all ages—Konstantyn hadn't thought to specify an age range—formed a line in front of the Cultural Club, a line modest in length but not in coloration. One middle-aged contestant sported a tweed suit, as though about to deliver a lecture; another contestant, around eleven or twelve, wore her newly starched school pinafore; another shivered in a strapless sequin gown, her wide-eyed toddler chewing the hem. And of course, there was Orynko Bondar, who opted for full folk: embroidered blouse, sheepskin vest, poppy-red skirt and boots, a headdress of wheat stalks that stuck out like sunbeams. The contestants shot embarrassed glances at one another to determine which of them had misinterpreted the dress code.

When the contestants' friends and relatives began showing up—not just from Kirovka but from the surrounding towns and villages—Konstantyn had begun to feel hopeful. His event would be well attended, his Cultural Club once again the center of activity. A beauty pageant would hardly be the pinnacle of the Club's achievements, but Konstantyn had to be patient. Poetry camps don't organize or fund themselves overnight.

On the Wednesday morning after the Minister's call came a special All Union First Radio program announcement. The same nasal voice that intoned Party proceedings and member passings informed Citizens that in eight weeks, in celebration of the mighty Union, an unprecedented event would take place: a Miss USSR beauty competition. Young women from every republic—aged sixteen to eighteen, in good moral standing—were invited to Moscow to take part, and the legitimate winner would be crowned at the Yuon Palace of Culture.

In his office, Konstantyn listened in disbelief. A *legitimate* winner. An *unprecedented* event. Either Konstantyn and his town—his country, even—were being punished, or attendance numbers at Moscow's many Palaces of Culture had been lagging, too. He was incensed that Irina Glebovna was both crushing the legitimacy of his pageant and copying it. True, he had copied it himself, from the Americans, who had probably copied it from the Europeans, but he had elevated the pageant to a more palatable level by enlisting a philosopher, a painter, a novelist, and an astronomer as judges.

Normally he would have laughed off the injustice, feeling above the government's antics; over dinner he would have regaled Milena with his droning impression of the radio announcer. But without Milena, without an audience, to laugh now felt pathetic, akin to drinking alone.

Konstantyn turned off the radio. The Cultural Club grew silent save for the shuffling footsteps in the hallway outside his office, then the jingle of a fifteen-kopek coin being pumped into Viktorina. He didn't want to imagine what would happen if the arcade game broke.

The phone rang again.

This time, Konstantyn picked up. It was the journalist, a bored-sounding woman with a smoker's rasp, still looking for that statement about Olga Bondar.

"Orynko Bondar," he corrected.

"Sure," the journalist said, clearly unhappy to have been assigned a story about some yokel town with ethnically named residents.

Konstantyn loosened the scarf around his neck, feeling hot. "Not only will Miss Kirovka be keeping her title," he heard himself declare, "but she'll be competing in the Miss USSR pageant." A dizzying array of possibilities opened within him. Yes, Miss Kirovka would go to Moscow. She would not be silenced. Finally he and his town would take pride in something other than the canning combine or the rumored silo under the sunflower fields. "Watch out for Orynko Bondar, representing Ukraine," he proclaimed, voice rising. "She will win over an entire empire."

On Thursday morning, upon arriving at the Cultural Club, Konstantyn discovered a man sitting in Konstantyn's swivel armchair, behind Konstantyn's oak desk. The surface of the desk had been cleared, the usual piles of documents replaced by a potted African violet.

The intruder's magnified eyes swam behind thick glasses. "Do you have an appointment?"

Konstantyn stood at his office door, kept his hand on the cold metal knob. "Do you?"

"Ah, Konstantyn Illych." The man, irritatingly young, hair slick with pomade, gave a tight smile, apparently embarrassed for them both. "Haven't you received the directive?" When Konstantyn shook his head, the man turned to the telefax machine, flipped through the pages hanging from its mouth, plucked one out, and handed it to Konstantyn. The curt letter informed the Director of the Kirovka Cultural Club of his termination.

Konstantyn focused his anger on the potted violet on the desk. He wanted to shred its chubby leaves. Instead, he reached forward and grabbed the phone, clamped it between his ear and shoulder—a gesture of importance, of expert phone handling. "If you'll excuse me." He didn't know what he would say to the Minister, exactly. The damage had been done.

Konstantyn nodded at the door, but the stranger didn't move.

"I'm sorry, Konstantyn Illych."

For a moment the men stared at each other. Both wore navy industrial-made suits. Konstantyn planted himself in the metal wire chair across from the desk. He had never sat in it before. The chair was angular, possessed bones of its own that poked up to meet the occupants, hurry them out of the office. He must have the chair replaced, he thought, before realizing this would no longer be in his power. He reread the letter and this time its contents sank in. His words came slowly: "I've worked here for twenty years. I'm a respected poet. Ten years ago I was named People's Artist."

His replacement gave him a pitying smile. The man's hand swept around the office, calling attention to the peeling wallpaper, the cracked ceiling—everything that no longer mattered.

The phone nestled in Konstantyn's lap beeped impatiently. Dial or hang up. He hung up.

The new Director busied himself. He pinched a dead leaf off the violet, pocketed it. He slid a document from a drawer and held it in front of his face. Konstantyn pretended to read the words and numbers on the other side of the sheet, hoping the action would render him useful again. The man's wedding ring drew his gaze. Konstantyn hadn't stopped wearing his own; it gave a man, especially one along in his years, legitimacy. If a man could keep a companion, surely there was nothing too wrong with him.

"Whether or not I work here, Orynko will compete for Miss USSR," Konstantyn vowed. What could he lose?

"I'm afraid," the man's soft voice came from behind the sheet, "the girl is gone."

"Gone?"

"Recruited by the Thermometric Academy. All thanks to your pageant. The girl had mentioned her desire to pursue thermophysical study, no?"

Orynko had indeed mentioned this during her onstage

interview, halfheartedly, to please her parents, who cheered her on from the front row. "I've never heard of any such academy," said Konstantyn.

"Me neither." The man replaced the document in the wrong drawer and looked toward the exit, likely wondering why Konstantyn still hadn't used it. "But I can assure you there is such a place."

Konstantyn had never felt less assured, but he played along. "I'm sure Orynko can leave for one pageant weekend."

"I'm sure, yes." He paused. "In theory."

Konstantyn adjusted himself in the torturous chair, suddenly worried.

"If the town where she is studying were to have road access," the man added, "and if the sea route hadn't just frozen over for the next eleven months."

Konstantyn gawked at him. "Where is this place? Siberia?"

The man remained still as a wax figure, neither confirming nor denying.

"No." Konstantyn was breathing quickly. Had the air suddenly thinned? "You can't just ship people to Siberia," he blustered, "not anymore."

"Certainly not. I am but a humble Cultural Director. What can people like us do?"

Unemployment was not kind to Konstantyn. He spent his days moping around his stuffy apartment, full of books that had once brought him joy but now mocked him, reminding him that the paltry few he'd written had grown just as dusty, yellowed, sour-smelling as the rest. He ate through his kitchen cabinets, went to bed early and woke late, but found little respite in sleep. His thoughts orbited Miss Kirovka, how it was his fault she was exiled, and that he hadn't a clue how to retrieve her. To make matters worse, while his provocation to the journalist had, predictably, been kept from the state media, his words had still somehow spread across town. Whenever he stepped outside for food or cigarettes—and only after counting and re-counting his cash savings—the benchers would accost him with questions. What would Orynko wear to the Miss USSR pageant, a squat bespectacled woman demanded to know. Was the girl taking singing lessons, a hook-nosed octogenarian inquired. Late one evening, when Konstantyn thought he was safe, a troupe of teenagers in neon windbreakers cheered at him from across the street. He tried to wave back but his hand grew limp, as if the tendons had been snipped. He couldn't bear to temper the townspeople's excitement, admit that they had, once again, nothing to hope for.

More and more, his wife's clothes haunted him. Blouses, trousers, sweaters spilled from drawers like shed skins. The nightgown he slept with exuded a smell he hadn't noticed before, spiced, herbal, as though he were a pest to repel.

Shirt by shirt, sock by sock, he began gathering his wife's effects into two cloth sacks. Somehow, wherever she was, she would surely feel him moving on, and the realization would hasten her return. He recalled when he was a boy, and he and his father would wait for his mother to come home from work, the dinner she'd made that morning reheated but cooling again. Only when they gave up and reached for their forks would she march in, as if she'd been at the door the entire time, testing their will. As Konstantyn folded away Milena's clothes, he couldn't help cocking his ear every few minutes, listening for the jangle of her keys. When he'd finished, he seated the cloth sacks on the sofa bed, unsure what to do with them. One never got rid of clothes—on the contrary, one spent every effort to acquire them in any size from near-empty shops, or saved them for gifts, or sewed them into different clothes, or, at the very least, repurposed them as rags. Banishing the clothes to his dacha wouldn't make enough of a statement, but he found he couldn't throw them away either, as this might anger Milena. Still, he was determined to go through the motions of closure. He would donate the clothes. The more obscure the cause, the more Milena would love him.

The car was borrowed, so Konstantyn took extra care as he drove along the muddy road. He wove over a hilly ridge, passed a rail yard, entered the forest. The orphanage hid deep inside it, 25 kilometers south of Kirovka.

It had rained the night before and the forest shone in the morning light. While it was a relief to briefly escape the town, to be anonymous again, Konstantyn felt a twinge of trepidation at what lay ahead. He had never visited Internat Number 12 before; the townspeople rarely spoke of it, as though fearful of invoking a ghost. But every time Konstantyn thought of turning back, the curtain of trees would part to reveal a breathtaking vista of hills and rivers; a squirrel would flash its golden tail in benediction; a butterfly would glint past in a streak of yellow and orange; and Konstantyn would remind himself that, after all, he was here to do good.

A cluster of cupolas peeked above the treetops. They appeared to have been skinned, with only the bulbous metal skeletons remaining. As he drove, the cupolas seemed to retreat into the distance, wary of the approaching stranger, but he soon caught up with them.

Internat Number 12, Konstantyn discovered, was an old monastery. The edifice sagged as if a great invisible hand were pressing on it from above. One of the towers had crumbled, its ruins laced with the roots of trees.

Konstantyn parked the rickety Zaporozhets alongside an iron fence. As he retrieved the first cloth sack from the trunk, he felt the weight of many eyes on the back of his neck. He gave a timid wave to the children watching him from arched windows. They kept still, as though painted onto the glass.

Finding the gates locked, Konstantyn turned to the small white box welded to a fence post, and pressed its red button. After a moment, a low staticky voice, a woman's, came on. "Yes?"

"I'd like to donate clothes." He said this loudly and clearly, as if his wife were hiding behind one of the pines, watching.

"You're from the Textile Union?"

"No."

"What's the organization?"

"Just a lone citizen."

After a pause, she asked, "What is it you want from us?"

He leaned in, thinking she had misheard. "I'm here to give clothing. To the children."

It was then he saw Orynko Bondar.

Or rather, a flash of Orynko Bondar, in another girl's face. One of the second-story windows was open, and a teenager rested her chin on the stone sill. Only her buzzed head was visible. Konstantyn thought she perfectly captured the vacant gaze of a fashion model. The orphan wasn't beautiful like Orynko, but there was something Orynko-ish in her—the dashes of the brows and lips, the jut of the jaw—as if an artist had tried to sketch the beauty queen in not-quite-sufficient light, using the nondominant hand.

"Leave the clothes by the gates," the woman instructed through the intercom. "I'll have someone pick them up."

Konstantyn set the sack down, but did not leave. He was still looking at the girl. Now he thought of the Greater Good. The Greater Good mattered most—wasn't that what he'd been taught his whole life? And so he could be forgiven a bit of deceit. He could slip the Orynko-ish girl into Orynko's place, to compete in the Miss USSR pageant. He would train her himself. In Moscow's vast Palace of Culture lectorium, each of the contestants would look no bigger than a pinkie finger onstage. Who could tell who was who, and who wasn't? As for the television broadcast: one could not overestimate the transformative effect of makeup, the distracting property of glitter. When Orynko had stepped onstage at the local pageant, her face powdered and painted, fake lashes flapping, she hadn't looked quite like Orynko either.

"I'd also like to foster a child," he announced, "for two months." He imagined the orphan's gratitude, and felt bolstered by it.

As the intercom rattled with instructions—forms to procure from the Ministry of Labor and Social Development, signatures to gather, and so on—Konstantyn gazed up, and thought he spotted the woman issuing them. At the fourth-floor window of the nearest tower, a broad-shouldered attendant in a white smock spoke into a phone.

"I'd like to proceed more quickly," he interrupted. "I'd be happy to leave the clothes here, but I'd also be happy to take them to another orphanage." He spoke to her as if she were his counterpart, without malice. They locked eyes in recognition, complicity. They both knew what it was to keep afloat an under-funded institution. Her tone softened. "You have a wife? It's not just you?"

"Not just me." The more he wanted it to be true, the less it felt like a lie.

"Your wife didn't come with you."

"She's preparing the extra room."

It seemed as if the attendant wanted this to be true, too. Her sigh crackled through the intercom. "Girl or boy?"

"How about—" Konstantyn feigned deliberation before pointing to the girl at the open window. "Her."

From her tower, the woman craned her neck out the window to look at the girl. The girl stared at nothing. For a terrible instant, Konstantyn thought she might be dead.

"I'll bring her right out," the attendant said quickly, her sudden enthusiasm unnerving. She retreated into the dark depths of the building.

A minute later the girl, too, was gone. The attendant appeared in her place, shut the window. Twenty minutes passed, thirty. Konstantyn considered ringing the intercom, but decided against it. Perhaps the girl was saying her goodbyes to the other children, who must be like brothers and sisters by this point. Perhaps she was tangled in their embraces, navigating the delicate terrain of their envy. Who was he to rush her? The longer he waited, the more he liked the girl.

At last the tall wooden doors of the monastery swung open. The attendant marched down the weedy brick path, pulling the orphan by the wrist. The girl struggled against the woman's grip, like a child who had just been woken. With her free hand she clutched a dusty pillowcase containing something bulky.

"No lice," the attendant promised, when the pair reached the iron gates. "You can see for yourself."

Up close, in full light, the teenager was not what he had envisioned. The arms and legs that stuck out of her baggy garment were very thin and pale, so pale they had a bluish glow. A thick white scar curdled her skin from nose to upper lip. This, combined with the buzzed head, the rough features, gave her a criminal look. And yet, once more Orynko flitted across the girl's face. This time the resemblance gave him a queasy feeling, recalled a shape-shifting octopus he had once seen on television, which survived its hostile habitat by mimicking anything from seaweed to a pile of poisonous snakes.

"Meet Zaya." The attendant pronounced the name like a challenge.

The girl regarded Konstantyn not with the timidity he expected of an orphan, but with a fierce intensity, as if she already knew Konstantyn and had decided long ago she disliked him.

Konstantyn felt his leg take a step back. He wanted to take another step, then another, until he reached the car and drove away. It took a momentous effort to twist his mouth into a smile. He leaned down to address the girl on the other side of the fence, but could not find anything to say. He had already forgotten her name.

The attendant unlocked the gates, ushered the orphan out, grabbed the sack of clothes Konstantyn had rested on the ground, clacked the gates shut. "Thank you for your kind donation. See you in two months."

When Konstantyn opened the trunk of the car, the girl drew back, as if he were about to throw her inside it. He gave a small high laugh. "It's for your things." He pointed at the remaining sack of his wife's clothes as an example (he had kept it back at the last moment for pageant needs). The girl gripped her bundle tighter to her chest. When he opened the passenger door, she made no move toward it. He rolled down the window, hoping this, too, would somehow prove the car's safety. He demonstrated getting in and out of the car while she watched, and thought he caught a cruel curl of her lip. He even suggested she walk beside the moving car as he held her hand—he feared she might run away—anticipating she would eventually tire and get in. But when he extended his hand, she struck it with the back of hers, hard. The orphan's strength alarmed him. When at last he threatened to drive away, leave her in that terrible place, she glowered at him, daring him to.

He sank behind the wheel but did not start the engine. With shaking, stinging fingers he tried to light a cigarette. On the fourth try he succeeded, and was about to take a grateful drag, when the cigarette left his lips.

The girl leaned in through the open passenger window. His cigarette hung from her mouth. She took a long, delicious pull before exhaling politely away from the car.

"I have more." He brandished the box, tapped the cartoon rocket shooting across its front. He hated himself for stooping so low.

At last the girl took the front seat. She sat her bundle on her lap.

During the drive, all conversation remained determinedly one-sided. Mostly, Konstantyn pointed at forest and meadow, saying, "See that big oak." "See that patch of daisies." "See those mushrooms, very poisonous." The girl kept her eyes on the muddy road.

He tried to ignore the smell of her, sweet and rank, like barley fermenting in urine. Keeping one hand on the wheel, he lit a second cigarette, inhaled. "Where'd you pick up the habit? From the older children?"

She shook her head.

"From the *sanitarki?*"

She nodded.

"You can talk to me. I don't bite."

She shot him a look: *I do.*

Konstantyn laughed; the girl did not. A rabbit dashed across the road. Her name came back to him. "What happened to your lip, Zaya?"

She said nothing.

"A bad fall," he guessed.

She shook her head.

"Thorny branch."

No.

"Fishhook."

No.

"Angry bird."

She took another pull. No.

"A three-headed dog you fought off valiantly."

No response.

"I thought so," said Konstantyn.

"An old *baba* sewed it up." The girl slurred her words. "She made leather boots."

Konstantyn winced. He didn't want to know more, but after a moment, he did. "This wasn't at the *internat?*"

She shook her head again. "I ran away, she took me in. Her hut burned down, she brought me back."

The forest receded. They drove between the sunflower fields

in silence. Soon Kirovka welcomed them with its bent metal sign framed by rusty braids of wheat. Konstantyn felt lighter. At least the girl could speak.

That night Konstantyn woke to a pinprick of orange light, felt nicotine breath on his face. He made out the girl's silhouette, bent over him. He jolted upright.

"Keep sleeping," she whispered.

He flicked on his reading lamp. No trace of Orynko in this girl's face. This stranger was wearing his wife's billowy dress shirt, which he'd lent her the evening before. She had brought no clothes of her own, had told him that her bundle contained only a saint, which had originally come with a hat before one of the other orphans stole it. A doll, not a saint, he assumed she'd meant.

"How long have you been sitting there?" he asked.

"Never seen a man sleep." She crossed one bare leg over the other, and stared at his mouth. "Odd, what lips are. Where you turn inside out."

Konstantyn tucked his lips between his teeth, protectively. The calm of her voice terrified him. She seemed capable of anything: she might break into dance or smash his skull with a skillet. He thought of the boot maker who had taken her in, could imagine the seed of the catastrophe: the girl gazing at a candle with the same cold fascination, wondering how the flame would look if it engulfed an entire house.

After that night he slept fitfully. He would wake up, listen for the girl's breathing, make sure that the breathing was at a suitable distance, that it came from the cot on the other side of the room, on the other side of the linen sheet he'd hung between them.

Of course, Konstantyn hadn't forgotten about the original Miss Kirovka. An encyclopedic search proved that the Thermometric Academy did indeed exist, in Norgorsk, deep within the Arctic Circle; the town was known for its smelting factory, which colored the snow pink, yellow, and black, and scented the air with chlorine and sulfur. In the early mornings, while the orphan slept, he wrote letters to Irina Glebovna and to the Chairman of Council of Ministers and his First Deputy Chairmen, State Committee Chairmen, and select members of the Presidium, calling for the beauty queen's repatriation. He'd received no response yet.

As for Miss Kirovka's double: before he could begin training her for the speech, the interview, the gown round, the bathing suit round—the radio announcement had not mentioned a talent round—the girl had to be caught up on the basics of civilized living. She never closed the bathroom door and he'd caught her squatting atop the toilet, feet on the seat. She balked at the idea of leg and armpit hair removal, saying that a buzzed head was enough to keep the lice away. She ate with agonizing slowness, inspecting each ingredient on her spoon with suspicion, yet she swallowed prune pits without a second thought. She feared the height of the balcony, and kept away from the windows. She slept with her dusty bundle at her side, refused to have it washed. She could recite the days of the week, but paid no heed to their order. If he thought he knew a subject, she probed him, out of curiosity or cruelty, until he reached the limits of his understanding. He could tell her about planets, how they were made of dirt or gas and moved in circles, but could not explain why they did so, only that gravity was involved. He couldn't tell her if time had a shape, or if the present and future could exist at once. She wanted to learn how a plane flies; he wanted her to learn to wash herself.

It took Konstantyn the first full month to broach the subject of the pageant. He led her to the park, where they sat on a pair of truck tires painted with polka dots. She no longer glared at strangers as if she wanted to maul them, which was no small improvement. The bundle lay at her side, appearing even dustier than usual in contrast to the pin-striped work shirt she was wearing (Konstantyn's). He divulged his plan: how she would be representing all of Ukraine as Miss Kirovka—more precisely, as Orynko Bondar, a girl who couldn't attend herself, although no one would know the difference. All Zaya had to do onstage, apart from twirl around in a pretty gown, was unfurl the sash emblazoned with MISS KIROVKA—he would make the sash himself, in whichever color she wanted—and wear Miss Kirovka's crown. An exact replica of the crown, rather. He told her about the judging panel of celebrated artists and Party members, about how every young woman dreamed of this kind of opportunity.

"I don't dream of it."

"Think of how pretty you'll be." He quickly added, "On top of how pretty you already are."

She watched a sparrow bathe in a murky puddle.

"You'll get to see Moscow. It's a hundred times bigger than Kirovka."

"This is why you came to the *internat*," she concluded. "Lucky me."

He swept his arm around the park, which was empty save for a few young mothers walking their strollers. "The country needs you."

The words had an effect on her, but not the one he'd intended. She stood up, and kicked the tire she'd been sitting on. "The *sanitarki* used to tell me, If you're so unhappy, send a letter to Brezhnev. And then it was Andropov, then Chernenko. They kept dying and we kept dying and I kept writing letters. Send a pair of stockings. Send iodine. I waited—not even a letter back. And now the country needs me." She pulled at the stiff collar of the work shirt, and set off in the direction of the apartment. He followed her, pleading. They were on the same side, he assured her, no one answered his letters either. But the girl marched on.

That night Konstantyn woke again. He listened for the girl's breathing, but heard only silence. He poked his head over the hanging sheet. Both the girl and the bundle were gone. They weren't in the kitchen or bathroom. He checked her cot again in the absurd hope he'd missed her the first time. He then stepped out onto the balcony, sick with panic. In the courtyard below, under the orange light of a streetlamp, he spotted the orphan squatting in an overgrown flower bed. She appeared to be digging. Her shoulder blades jutted out through her nightgown like the stumps of wings. The loyal bundle lay at her side. When he called her name, she froze for a second, then resumed digging with renewed vigor. He didn't want to approach her any more than he would a feral animal, but reminded himself that, regrettably, she was his charge. So he stuffed his feet into a pair of loafers, and raced down the concrete steps.

The girl didn't look up when Konstantyn reached her.

She had already dug an impressive hole using a flat stone. He demanded an explanation, but she gave none. When he begged her to come back inside, she ignored him. He took hold of her arm; she screamed. His hand jerked away as if scalded.

Several stories above, a window slammed shut.

For some time, Konstantyn watched her dig. If he were her father, he wondered whether he would know what to do. People with children always seemed to know.

A tuft of yellow hair poked out from the pillowcase. It looked remarkably real. Konstantyn sat on his haunches, pulled back the fabric. A face squinted up at him, brown and shriveled. Not a doll—human. Very dead. Oddly short. "What did you do?" he stammered at the girl, as though she had just murdered the thing, hacked half of it off, and was attempting to bury the evidence.

She grabbed a broken beer bottle by its neck, and brandished it at Konstantyn. He tipped backward.

"Use this," she explained. She was worn out, her breathing heavy.

It was then that Konstantyn felt something inside him melt. The bottle was not meant to be a threat—the girl was asking for help. For the first time, Konstantyn found he was not repulsed by her. He could sympathize with her as he was supposed to. Bolstered by his newfound virtue, he slowly reached for the broken bottle, the fragile offering. He began to dig alongside the orphan, averting his eyes from the mummified creature—"a saint," he remembered now. Not wishing to spoil the moment, he posed no further questions.

The night sky faded to a grayish green. When the girl stopped digging, so did he. With great care she lowered the bundle into the pit, which they then refilled with dirt. She pressed the fresh earth with her palms, and pulled dried weeds over it like a blanket.

They sat beside each other on the edge of the flower bed, silent. The girl's usual scowl had softened. She regarded the *novostroïki* enclosing the courtyard as though they had done something to disappoint her.

"Pageant or no pageant," she said in her slurring voice, "you want to take me back to the *internat*." There was no plea in her tone, only resigned observation. Konstantyn couldn't bring himself to lie. As he fumbled for the right words, she spoke again. "I'll go to Moscow."

This surprised him. He hadn't expected her to change her mind. "You'll run away."

"Already tried. I'll just end up back at the *internat*."

"Then why?"

She scraped dirt from under her nails. "Why not."

"We have three weeks. A lot of work ahead of us."

The orphan gave Konstantyn a searing smile. Her teeth were nightmarishly crooked, as though she had stuck them in herself as a toddler. "I'm your girl."

After that night, Zaya became surprisingly agreeable. She ate whatever Konstantyn cooked with a methodical determination: fatty cutlets, greasy stews, fried potatoes and pork rinds doused in sour cream. She plodded through tongue twisters to sharpen her diction. She attempted to straighten her teeth by pressing on them with the back of a spoon. She spent the crisp spring afternoons tanning her towel-wrapped self on the balcony—smoking dulled her fear of heights—and her bluish pallor gave way to a soft buttermilk. (Zaya still considered the issue of bodily hair moot, but Konstantyn made peace with this, not wanting to strain the fragile alliance.) To practice pivoting in heels, she wobbled around the apartment in a pair of velvet pumps Konstantyn found at the back of the closet—Milena's, surely, though he'd never seen her wear them. Konstantyn borrowed a silvery wig from a neighbor who had worn it during chemotherapy, and Zaya pulled it onto her shorn head and flicked the locks over her shoulders, like the actresses she observed on television. She rehearsed the speech he'd written for her: "My name is Orynko Bondar, from Kirovka, Ukraine," she would begin. Though Konstantyn felt strange hearing her use another's name, Zaya herself seemed unfazed, as though identity were nothing more than a hat she could slip on and off. "I love the sea and the smell of rain," she would chant at him. "I love animals, especially dogs." She would exclaim, "Beauty will save the world," almost as if she believed it.

For the gown round, Konstantyn unearthed a mustard-yellow dress with extra-wide bishop sleeves that gathered into elastic cuffs, gifted to Milena from his mother for their marriage registration.

Konstantyn fashioned the crown and sash replicas from the same materials he'd used for the originals: a three-liter tin can dipped in glitter, a polyester only-for-guests tablecloth. Zaya practiced the grand reveal. Upon reaching the end of the catwalk (corridor), she slid the crown and sash from her sleeves, put them on, pretended to bask in the applause, and strutted back.

The bathing costume, also Milena's, was a thick wool tunic with knee-length bloomers, possibly procured from the Victorian era. Bloated with ruffles and pleats, the garment perplexed both Zaya and Konstantyn. "Even if I knew how to swim, I'd drown in this thing," she said the first time she donned it. Konstantyn, however, appreciated the full coverage. Though his own pageant had included a bathing suit round, he felt a moral discomfort about the impending one in Moscow. He did not like to imagine the leering eyes of the entire Union on the contestants, and on this contestant in particular, whose qualities could not be assessed by mere stage light.

The more Konstantyn occupied himself with training Zaya, the less he thought about his wife. One hour, two hours, would pass by without Milena flitting through his mind. When he woke in the morning, he no longer had to remind himself why she was not lying beside him.

"What's the one thing people don't know about you?"

Zaya stood atop a chair, her makeshift stage, holding a wooden spoon as a microphone. They hadn't rehearsed this interview question before. "What people?"

"Friends, family." He'd uttered the second word without thinking. She let him wallow in his own shame for a moment. "People at the *internat*," he amended.

"You can't take a squat there without an audience. Everyone knows everything about everyone."

"Some hidden talent," he ventured. "A secret wish."

Zaya peeled off her wig, rubbed her bristly scalp. The effect of the rich stews was beginning to show: no longer did shadows fill her cheeks, hang from her jutting collarbones. She resembled the teenage boys who roamed the neighborhood at night, scrawny but not skeletal.

"Sometimes I wish I'd never learned to talk," she told him. "What's the point?"

"We're talking now, aren't we?"

She nodded at the window. "But out there it's dead space. No use running your tongue because who listens? It's worse to know it." She turned back to him. "But I can't say that at the pageant."

If it were up to him, he wanted to assure her, she could. Instead, he said, "The judges want something hopeful."

"Hopeful." Zaya flashed a plastic smile. "How about a poem?" She lifted the microphone-spoon to her lips, launched into a recitation. "Belts bearings cab chassis / Decals duals dewy in the sun / Engine hitch . . ."

It took a moment for Konstantyn to recognize the poem as one of his own. What were meant to be free-flowing lines, carried by intuition and inspiration, were chopped up, forced into the metered lilt of a nursery rhyme. He'd been proud of that poem, how it concluded with the setting sun painting the metals red—a delicately hidden representation of rust, or societal decay. Now the words made him cringe.

"I read it in one of your books last night, while you were asleep," Zaya said. "But I already knew it. A *sanitarka* used it to teach us tractor parts."

"Tractor parts!" He found himself yelling. "It isn't *about* tractor parts."

Zaya descended from the chair and slumped down into it, arms hanging between thighs. Her expression was mean and satisfied; the insult had hit its mark.

"Sit up straight." He threw back his shoulders as an example, to no effect. "The *sanitarki* taught you tractor parts but not the order of the days of the week?"

"Want me to recite the one about gears?"

He put out a hand to stop her. He realized he preferred to think no one read his poetry anymore.

Makeup proved to be a challenge. Konstantyn hoped that, by virtue of being a girl, Zaya held some innate ability to apply it. From the depths of the bathroom cabinet he dug out a nub of lipstick, a tiny jar of flesh-colored paste, a tube of mascara—remnants from the rare times he and his wife had gone out. He placed the objects on the kitchen table, in front of Zaya. She uncapped the mascara, smelled the unsheathed brush. He realized she hadn't a clue what it was.

"To darken your eyelashes. Let me," he offered, taking the brush. He instructed her to look up at the ceiling, open her mouth.

"Why?"

He didn't know. It was how his wife had always arranged her face to apply mascara. "Just don't blink." But when he brought the brush to her eye, she threw her head back as though he held a weapon. He tried again, with the same result.

"Do it to yourself first," she ordered.

"It's not for me."

She crossed her arms. "You have eyelashes."

He sighed, and held up the compact mirror. He watched himself bring the brush to his right eye. The lashes were thin and straight and stuck downward. He'd never paid attention to them before. He applied the clumpy purplish black paste. A few times he missed, and grazed his eyelid. He tried to wipe the marks off but ended up smearing them further, giving himself a black eye.

"See? Nothing to it." He smiled meekly, holding up his hands to prove he was unarmed.

Zaya leaned in to study his work. Her brown irises were flecked with amber, like sparks about to ignite. He cast down his eyes to avoid them. To his relief, she took the brush, but instead of using it on herself she lifted it to his left eye. Now he was the one who wanted to squirm from the brush. He willed himself to keep still, to show that he trusted her even though he didn't, not quite.

As she worked, the heel of her hand rested on his cheek like a cool stone. He held his breath, immobilized by her touch. He tried to remember when he had last been in such proximity to another person, and his mind slid back in time, trying and failing to latch onto some distant memory.

"Your eyes are all wet," she remarked.

"Must be mascara in them."

"Sorry," she said. "It's leaking." She pressed the back of her hand against his cheek to catch it.

"How do I look?" he asked.

"Like Miss USSR." She handed over the brush. "Just don't take my eye out."

They proceeded this way, taking turns with the eye shadow—a metallic powder that clung to the mascara like mold—and the lipstick, which exuded a waxy fragrance, faintly petrochemical.

This left the foundation. He suspected he had mixed up the order of operations. He opened the jar of paste, which contained a circular sponge. When it was his turn, he dabbed it over Zaya's face haphazardly. The color was a shade pinker than her skin, but the effect wasn't bad—it made her face seem flushed, a tad more alive. When he passed over the thick scar below her nose, she flinched. He could see white specks where the boot maker's needle had pierced the skin; the strokes had been quick and indelicate. Since the woman had taken the time to sew up a child's face, he thought with a pang of anger, why not take a few extra minutes to do it well? If he had been there—

The thought went unfinished. He hadn't been there. He wouldn't have taken in the child, in the first place.

He and Zaya stood in front of the bathroom mirror, appraising the colors on their faces. Their shadowy eyes and smeared lips made them looked vaguely related.

The next day, Zaya and Konstantyn took a two-car *elektrichka* from Kirovka to Kiev, then an overnight train to Moscow. Zaya's distrust of cars did not seem to extend to other forms of transportation. In fact, it was Konstantyn who was nervous, breaking out in a sweat every time the conductor made rounds to check tickets. Once or twice, on previous trips, Konstantyn had seen men asked to provide a birth certificate for an accompanying child or teenager. Yet no one questioned him. Perhaps when the conductors saw the young woman sitting beside him, long silver locks spilling from her fur hood, heeled boot pumping impatiently, they assumed she was related to him, and not by blood. When they arrived in Moscow the next morning, the arched iron and glass roof of the Kievsky Terminal slid over them like a long net.

The Yuon Palace of Culture was a granite amalgamation of angles and planes, as if a committee of architects had failed to agree on a single design and so combined several. Konstantyn and Zaya edged along the Palace's jagged perimeter until they came to a back door. Locked, as expected. But within a few minutes a rotund middle-aged man rushed out clutching a broken stiletto, and the pair slipped inside.

Chaos greeted them in the narrow corridor. People were running about, barking commands at one another. A heavily made-up teenager in a white slip, undoubtedly one of the contestants, limped in circles, sobbing. Another girl, hair set in pink rollers, was dry-heaving over a dustbin. Konstantyn observed, with some satisfaction, that no one seemed to know what they were doing or where they should go. It was true that his pageant had been much smaller, but its lead-up had been incomparably calmer, better organized.

He kept an eye out for the Minister of Culture, for the wide-jawed, handsome face that occasionally graced television broadcasts and newspapers. Konstantyn suspected, and hoped, she wouldn't condescend to oversee the tedious backstage details.

As they pushed through the corridor, Konstantyn caught envious glances at Zaya's thinness. A tall blonde, who was slicking Vaseline onto the teeth of her daughter—a taller, blonder version of herself—asked Zaya which diet she kept. "The *internat* diet," Zaya answered. The mother turned away, as if the girl had uttered a curse word.

A small, quick-moving woman with a glossy folder clamped under her arm intercepted Zaya and Konstantyn.

"Changing room?" he tried.

The woman shot Zaya a disapproving glance. "All contestants are accounted for."

When Konstantyn asked if it wasn't possible to accommodate another, the administrator said of course it wasn't possible, these girls had been vetted in their respective republics before being sent here from all over the Union. Konstantyn probed his mind for useful people he knew, or could pretend he knew; it occurred to him that one of the judges was a composer who, according to the lore of the intelligentsia, coded his favorite granddaughter's name into his music. Konstantyn invoked that name now, in diminutive form, as if he personally knew her. Surely the granddaughter—and by extension, her famous grandfather, and by extension, the Minister of Culture—would be crushed if the girl's best friend was not allowed to compete? The administrator stared at Konstantyn with indignation. He knew the woman didn't believe him, but he also knew she wouldn't be willing to risk the chance his story was true. She pulled her folder out from under her arm and opened it. "You're in luck," she conceded, "we had a contestant pull out after she twisted her knee." She unclipped a pen from her shirt collar, and turned to Zaya. "Age?"

Zaya looked blank.

"Sixteen," Konstantyn intervened. This was Orynko's age.

"Engaged or married?"

Zaya shook her head.

"Children?"

"What about them?"

"Do you have any, or are you expecting."

"She's sixteen," Konstantyn repeated.

"If she bleeds between the legs it's possible."

"I don't bleed between the legs," said Zaya.

Both Konstantyn and the administrator turned to her in surprise. The subject had never come up, but Konstantyn had assumed it was because Zaya was tending to it on her own, stoically, the way women did.

The administrator ticked something on her page. Seeing the look on Konstantyn's face, she said, "I don't make the questions." At last she asked Zaya, "Name and provenance?"

"My name is Orynko Bondar, from Kirovka, Ukraine," the girl announced, in a stage voice Konstantyn wished she'd save for the stage. He tensed, the gravity of the moment settling on his shoulders like a lead coat. The original Orynko Bondar had been carted away hundreds of kilometers to prevent her from being here today, from uttering those simple words. Konstantyn was ready to pull out a small envelope of cash in case the administrator recognized Miss Kirovka's name and refused to add it, but it appeared that no such directive had trickled down to her. "How about a stage name? Something a tad more"—the woman paused, choosing her words—"urban."

Something a tad more Russian, he knew she'd meant. "We're keeping the name."

The administrator shrugged, recorded the name, and opened the dressing room door for the new contestant. Fumes of aerosols, eaux de toilette, and singed hair burst forth, as did the sounds of spraying, peeling, and other torturous acts. The administrator rushed down the corridor to tend to the girl with the hair rollers, who had begun retching again.

Zaya and Konstantyn stood at the doorway. He could accompany her no further. He was supposed to hand off the suitcase with the marriage-registration dress, bathing costume, makeup, crown, and sash, but found himself unable to do so. The dressing room threw a cold, cutting light on Zaya's skin. He had an urge to yank her away from it, reverse his horrid plan. He could no longer convince himself that, once the face of Miss Kirovka's double was broadcast around the Union, she would be safe. After all, he had not been able to predict Orynko's exile.

"You don't have to do this," he blurted. "We can turn around, go home."

With that last word, "home," the future rearranged itself in a splendid vision. His home would be hers, too. He'd sleep on a cot in the corridor, give her the entire room. Never would the girl suffer again. He'd enroll her in school, a good school, where she would be surrounded by knowledgeable people—much more knowledgeable than Konstantyn—who would teach her about the dynamics of flight, planetary orbits, anything she had ever wondered about.

"Kostya," she said softly, "I'm living out a girl's dream." Her face was closed to him, as though she were already gone. She took the suitcase, stepped into the dressing room.

The Palace of Culture lectorium dwarfed the one in Kirovka. Its four curved balconies hummed with spectators waiting for the show to begin. A red runner carpet—the catwalk—bisected the stage. To the right a television crew hustled around a nest of cables. To the left stood the judges' table, the six brass name-plates designating the seats waiting to be filled: MINISTER OF CULTURE, CHAIRMAN OF COUNCIL OF MINISTERS, STATE COM-MITTEE CHAIRMAN, PROCURATOR GENERAL, PAINTER, COM-POSER. Snatches of melody rose from the narrow orchestra pit, where the musicians were warming up.

Konstantyn sat in the second row, main level. He was so close to the stage, he could smell its newly varnished floor. He tried to let himself sink into the cheerful chatter around him. He envied the other spectators their simple motive for being here—to enjoy themselves, watch a good show.

The lights dimmed. An oboist blew a piercing note, joined by the woodwinds, brass, strings, timpani. Konstantyn had heard an orchestra tune only a handful of times in his life and, despite his nervousness, the sound of the instruments joining in a single voice made him shiver with pleasure.

A small bearded man in a burgundy suit—an actor whose name Konstantyn couldn't remember—stepped onto the stage and the hall burst into applause. He welcomed everyone to the Miss USSR beauty competition, the first of its kind in the Union ("Second," Konstantyn muttered), and reminded the audience of the prizes to be claimed: a victory tour around the Union, a large-screen television, and a white dress. The orchestra played the city's anthem as the judges filed in and found their seats, solemn faces fit for a court proceeding. Irina Glebovna was the last to enter the stage. She wore a brown pantsuit with thick, armor-like shoulder pads, and her skin possessed the yellowish sheen of the embalmed. Before taking a seat, she installed herself in front of the announcer's microphone and gave a spirited speech about the importance of a Union glued together not only by a common economy and language, but also by a common culture—three components guaranteeing peace, to be enjoyed by many generations to come.

The pageant opened with the gown round. The thirty-five contestants waited at the far end of the stage, a row of silhouettes in the dim lighting. When called, each stepped into the spotlight, and strutted down the runway holding a white paper fan labeled with a number. Unlike the hodgepodge of contestants in Konstantyn's pageant, the young women here had a uniform look: pastel gowns, teased hairstyles, aggressive teeth-and-gums smiles.

Contestant Number 14, from Turkmenistan, bobbed a curtsy at the end of the runway.

Contestant Number 18, from Georgia, blew a kiss.

Finally the announcer called, "Orynko Bondar from Kirovka, Ukraine!"

The Minister of Culture straightened in her seat. She raised an index finger to the camera crew in warning: Be ready to cut.

Zaya marched in front of the Party members, the spotlight trailing her like a blazing eye. She wore makeup so thick it looked creamy, like something that needed refrigeration—an administrator's doing, he assumed. Zaya's puffy sleeves—decades out of style, Konstantyn saw now—bulged with the crown and sash. Did he still want her to put them on? He tried to catch her eye, but on she trooped, one high-heeled foot in front of the other. She appeared unshaken by the size of the audience, gazing straight ahead as if walking a tightrope. In one moment Konstantyn felt himself rising in his seat, ready to snatch her from the stage's deep maw; the next, he egged the girl on: show them, Miss Kirovka, show them that neither you, nor your townspeople, nor your country, will be silenced.

At last she reached the end of the runway. And—nothing happened. Instead of revealing the crown and sash, she simply turned on her heel and strode back upstage, as if this had been the plan all along.

Konstantyn felt dizzy with relief. He was grateful for her disobedience. Had the spectators recognized the name? Had they caught the significance of Miss Kirovka's presence?

Zaya rejoined the line of silhouettes. As the other contestants continued to file down the runway, domestic worries filled Konstantyn's mind, thrilling in their newness. He thought of the shoes and coat Zaya would need for the upcoming winter, the schoolbooks he would have to procure.

His attention was wrenched back to the stage at the word "Norgorsk." The twenty-first contestant stepped under the spotlight. Orchestral music swelled as she glided down the runway in an opal mermaid gown and a white fur shawl that glowed under the lights. Her silvery hair had been teased and crimped into a leonine mane. Konstantyn thought he had never seen someone so breathtaking, but as she approached, he realized he had.

It was Orynko Bondar. This time, the real Orynko Bondar.

Konstantyn watched in disbelief. The name the announcer had called couldn't have been hers—Konstantyn would have caught it. She had been given a stage name, he figured, something more *urban*. He searched Orynko's face for signs of trauma. She looked older, perhaps, her features settling into their adult state, but whatever trials she'd undergone during her exile seemed to have left no mark. She'd returned to her first home—the stage. She flapped her fan around her shoulders like a dove, to roaring applause. Charmingly bashful, she waved at the audience, as though she'd personally invited each one of them and couldn't believe they'd all come.

Konstantyn turned to look at Irina Glebovna. Was this her doing? Was she using Orynko, the seasoned contestant, for some nefarious end? But Irina Glebovna seemed just as surprised as Konstantyn by the original Miss Kirovka's reappearance. The Minister's expression wavered between wonder and anguish as she watched her grand pageant fade away. Later that evening, Konstantyn would learn the truth from Orynko herself: the remote Norgorsk also had a Cultural Club and its director had insisted, upon discovering her, that she represent the town. The smelting factory boasted its own private airport, and the rest had fallen into place.

Konstantyn sat on his hands, trying to contain his excitement. He couldn't imagine a happier ending to the evening.

The moment the pageant ended he would seek out Orynko and Zaya, and the three of them would return to Kirovka.

It was a pretty thought. Konstantyn held on to it even when, minutes later, between the twenty-fifth and twenty-sixth contestants, Zaya kicked off her pumps and broke from the line. She crossed the stage at a slow, deliberate pace, impervious to the unease passing through the other contestants. She stopped in front of the judges' table. As she considered the Party members one by one, they blinked back at her, shifted in their seats. The Procurator General, white-haired with opulent jowls, leaned toward the girl in the quaint yellow dress, ready to receive her message.

The audience fell silent then, ready for her message, too. The last chords of the orchestral piece hung in the air, and the conductor looked up from the pit to the announcer, unsure whether to continue. The twenty-sixth contestant, a tall Estonian in a gauzy dress, halted midstrut.

"If you could keep the runway circulation moving," the announcer told the Estonian.

Go back, Konstantyn mouthed to Zaya, his lips still curled in a frozen smile. Go back go back. She stood just a few meters away from where he sat—he could see the tip of her ear poke through her wig. If only she would turn to him.

Irina Glebovna sat very still.

Konstantyn could just make out Zaya's words. "You never answered my letters."

The wet lips of the Procurator General parted into a grin meant for a small child. He said something Konstantyn couldn't hear. Zaya flicked her chin up. The Procurator General jerked back, his mouth open. He touched his cheek.

It took Konstantyn a moment to realize that she had spat on him. The hall erupted in gasps, jeers.

Irina Glebovna made a slicing motion at the camera crew.

Now the State Committee Chairman twisted back, as if slapped.

As Zaya was sucking in her cheeks, drawing up saliva for a third attack, two men in uniform entered the lectorium from a side door. For a moment Zaya watched them approach, her face slack and her eyes deadened—the way they had been back at the *internat,* Konstantyn remembered. She seemed ready to accept whatever punishment these men threatened; it could be no worse than the one she had already been dealt.

Konstantyn sprang to his feet. He tore down the row of seats, treading on polished shoes and pedicured toes, and bounded up the steps to the stage as the guards closed in on Zaya. When her eyes met Konstantyn's, she jolted awake. Her lithe body slipped from the guards' hands, and she raced to the edge of the stage, toward the audience. Konstantyn glimpsed the pink underside of her foot as she launched herself into the air, leaping over the orchestra pit. For a moment he feared she wouldn't clear it, imagined the pit sucking her in. Her dress parachuted out as she landed—to Konstantyn's relief—in the carpeted space between the pit and the first row of petrified spectators. She took a second or two to steady herself, before she bolted up the aisle, heading for the exit.

"Konstantyn Illych?" Orynko shouted from the row of contestants.

Konstantyn reeled around. He could not let Orynko out of his sight now, lest she disappear again. He ran to her, grabbed her by the wrist, and set off after Zaya. The girl was already halfway across the lectorium, weaving between the spectators crowding into the aisle. A mustachioed man tried in vain to catch her. Konstantyn cursed the crowd, but was grateful for the added commotion, which sheltered him, and the contestant he had just whisked offstage, from the guards. By the time Konstantyn, still pulling Orynko in his wake, had waded to the exit, he'd lost track of Zaya. Outside, a bitter wind dashed between the tall stone buildings, slapped his and Orynko's faces. He thought he saw a streak of yellow, and ran after it. But one cavernous street opened up to another, unfolding endlessly.

"My feet hurt," Orynko protested, struggling to keep up in her stilettos. Passersby gawked at her, an apparition from another world. "Can't we go home?"

"One more street," Konstantyn promised. "Just one more."

As they searched, he thought of the moment Zaya had last looked at him, onstage. He conjured the expression on her face over and over, but each time her gaze changed. In one version, she was charmed but confused by the sight of Konstantyn racing toward her, calling her name as though she were the one who would save him; in another version, she struggled to remember who he was; in another, her face regained life and she found something to run for—Konstantyn, and their shared future. This was the version he held on to, in the years to come.

Orynko Bondar's homecoming was magnificent. The townspeople filled the platform of the Kirovka train station, and applauded as Orynko and Konstantyn descended the steep steps of the passenger car. Never before had Konstantyn seen such a crowd in his town. He hadn't slept the whole trip back. His eyes were red, heavy-lidded. Strangers slapped his back, shook his limp hand. He wished they would all go away.

Orynko's parents—short-haired, wearing practical foot-wear—wrapped themselves around the teenager, kissed her face. Konstantyn heard her father whisper in her ear, "But the Academy!" A small boy in a dress shirt thrust a bouquet of pink dahlias into Orynko's hands. A canister of home brew made the rounds.

Brave girl, foolish girl, the townspeople exclaimed. When had Miss Kirovka learned to spit with such aim, such force? From this, Konstantyn understood that the broadcast of the Moscow pageant had cut out right after Zaya spat on the judges. He found himself enraged at the townspeople. How could they have mistaken Zaya for Orynko, when she was so obviously Zaya? How could they have failed to recognize the real Orynko as the contestant from Norgorsk? Had the camera not zoomed in on the girls' faces, or had the townspeople simply wanted to believe the impossible? His convoluted plan had succeeded, and he hated himself for it.

Her name is Zaya, he wanted to shout, Zaya from Internat Number 12. An adept sprinter, a reciter of poems.

But now the townspeople pressed around Orynko and Konstantyn. They took Orynko's reticence for modesty, Konstantyn's red eyes for fatigue. As the pair stumbled out of the station, the crowd followed, boisterous as a victory parade.

PART
TWO

==

After
the
Fall

LUCKY TOSS

I'd been working as a guard at the saint's tomb for eighteen months before the trouble began. Konstantyn Illych paid me little but provided free lodging—an army cot and stove I could fold out in the corner of the tomb each night. The job consisted of telling pilgrims to keep hands out of pockets and lips off the display case. Sometimes children rapped the glass, bored by the saint's inactivity, and I would remind them that we were not a zoo.

The saint's display case, which Konstantyn Illych bought from a defunct delicatessen shop at quarter price, boasted a curved glass front and a steel ledge with tracks for plastic trays. Normally the saint basked under the fluorescent lamp like a glazed roast, but that particular day the bulb began to flicker, making the creature look as though it were twitching awake. At first the effect pleased Konstantyn Illych, who wanted the crowd of pilgrims to grow even thicker, but after the second pilgrim fainted he asked me to procure a replacement bulb—though not before we closed the tomb, at 18:30.

The tomb was a low-ceilinged concrete room in the crumbling building known as 1933 Ivansk. The room was bare as a bunker, containing only the display case, a narrow counter for the cash register, and a small bathroom (not for public use).

Before being a tomb it had been a hair salon and before that, a ground-level suite. The owner of the salon had knocked out the street-facing wall and replaced it with glass panes. When Konstantyn Illych bought the space, he knocked out the inner walls, too, to make room for the pilgrims. That the rest of 1933 Ivansk had not yet collapsed on us almost made me believe in the saint.

I'd approached Konstantyn Illych about the position after the Union fell and job prospects plummeted. He had already fired two guards for their substandard work ethic. Despite our unfortunate history—the letter of apology he never wrote or signed—we had reached a truce; I blamed him for ruining my career at the agency, and he blamed his failed marriage on the distress I'd caused, and so we were even. Even, but not equal, and Konstantyn Illych enjoyed reminding me of this fact: as my new boss he reveled in assigning me pointless tasks, such as dusting the insides of locks and buffing the stainless steel screws of the display case. I'd reached a similarly uneasy peace with Milena Markivna, who had returned to the building but not to Konstantyn Illych. For the past few months she'd been living on the ninth floor with a stylish young woman named Larissa and her two daughters, but Konstantyn Illych's repeated assertions that the women were merely roommates made me suspect they were more. Of course, I dared not ask Milena Markivna myself. The only time she and I had spoken since her return, she'd joked that I had finally realized my dream of becoming an Honor Guard. But I sensed my presence embarrassed her—I was a sticky residue from a past she longed to forget.

Most of the tomb's visitors were women and children. They laid portraits of men atop the display case. When the town's canning combine had closed, the men had taken to the sunflower fields, drinking cheap perfumes with flip-top caps, the brightly colored bottles shaped like grenades. Now, every evening, the men's portraits rustled like dead leaves as I swept them away.

We permitted photography inside the tomb. Konstantyn Illych believed it helped spread the word. Visitors loved snapping close-ups of the saint's teeth, a speckless set of ivories better preserved than any other saint's and certainly than any Kirovkavite's, dead or living. We townspeople all carried stomatological trauma, our mouths junk heaps of lead fillings, wire bridges, steel crowns, plastic prostheses. When the pilgrims peered into the saint's mouth—eternally thrown open, a model patient—they must have been transported to a happier time.

Most of the attention in the tomb centered on the saint, but on occasion I'd catch a pair of eyes on me. A glint of recognition, and perhaps contempt. Likely I imagined this. When the newspapers had begun publishing lists of names from declassified archives, I'd searched for mine but had not seen it. I did find an ex-colleague's name, from the agency. He must have found it, too—or worse, his family had. The next time his name appeared in the paper, it was to announce that he had hanged himself, "unable to bear the burden of his crimes." He had been much older than I, had operated in a different time. My tasks had been confined to the desk, and I'd never wielded anything larger than a pen.

Spotlights, striplights, pot lights, floodlights. There are myriad ways to illuminate a delicatessen display case, I learned at the hardware tent at the bazaar.

Most of the concrete storefronts sat empty, as they had before the Union's collapse, but the tents of the bazaar now sprawled ten blocks, selling anything from cow hooves to floppy disks. These tents sprouted and folded at an alarming speed; if one waited too long, it was impossible to find the same vendor twice. I hated this place, with its tantalizing colors and wafts at ever-inflating prices. I always came away feeling poorer, even if I hadn't spent a single *kupon*. The conundrum of former times—having money with nothing to spend it on—had been cruelly inverted.

"Are you displaying meat or fish?" the hardware sales boy yelled at me over the rattle of the electric generator by his feet. "Pastries? Greens?" He looked about fourteen and smelled of pomade. Behind him, a wall of shelves gleamed with a dizzying array of light fixtures. A few blinked and/or changed colors.

I didn't want to explain. "Meat."

"Fresh or cured?"

"Cured."

The sales boy warned against fluorescent bulbs, which made meat look blue; high-UV lights drained flesh to an unlively gray; incandescent bulbs promoted rotting. He insisted on halogen, which reacted with tungsten and brought out meat's natural blush. To demonstrate, he posed his face beside a bulb shaped like a tiny satellite dish. Indeed, a before-unseen pimple on his chin glowed a freshly squeezed red. "A halogen bulb sells your product for you," he assured.

A halogen bulb cost two hundred *kupony* and Konstantyn Illych had given me fifty.

"A regular bulb will do," I said.

The boy puckered his lips, now crimson, as if painted with lipstick. "A halogen bulb pays for itself," those lips promised.

When I showed the boy my lone bill, his enthusiasm wilted. Again I missed the years when one had fewer choices, fewer ways to disappoint.

—

The next day I woke at dawn. Konstantyn Illych had instructed me to change the bulb before the crowds of pilgrims arrived outside the tomb and gathered along the glass wall, so as not to detract from the mystique of the saint. I had several times suggested installing curtains to pull over the glass, but Konstantyn Illych said he did not have the money. I doubted this was true. All those coins, warm from pilgrim palms, must have amounted to a weighty sum. And I knew Konstantyn Illych was currently renovating his suite nine stories above. He had wedged an extra room into it, for his runaway foster child. She'd been gone for over a year, but Konstantyn Illych awaited the girl like the pilgrims awaited their savior. He'd even bought her a new wardrobe, in four different sizes, anguished that he couldn't know how much she had grown.

I unlocked the saint's display case, slid open its rear door. The smell of oil and dirt burst forth, as if something had been uprooted from the parched earth. I tried to unscrew the spent bulb, contorting my arms to avoid grazing the body, but the bulb had fused to its rusty socket. I could not work while the saint remained inside the case.

I paused and considered the wretched creature: legless, not much larger than a toddler, it screamed at me soundlessly, brown skin taut around its lipless mouth. Konstantyn Illych had told me that the saint belonged to his foster child, but not how she'd gained possession of it, and I had no desire to inquire further.

Things I'd have rather touched: a lamp full of dead insects, swamp scum, the raw cavern of an alley cat's ear, the slimy inside of a toilet plunger in a public bathroom that had run out of soap. I could have spent the morning bargaining against my fate, if only there had been someone to bargain with.

(I had watched the pilgrims trying to bargain with the saint all the time. They would bend over the glass, inspecting the saint's nostrils, eyes, ears, for bleeding. Rumors had circulated about the saint's powers—Tinnitus, soothed! Eczema, cleared! Drinking habit, broken!—but I did not believe them. To me the saint seemed wholly occupied by its century-long scream. Or yawn. I could never decide which.)

I averted my eyes from the mouth, and considered the saint's torso, hips, the bluish twist of robes where the legs would have been. I wondered if these limbs had broken off postmortem, when the catacombs were ravaged. If the saint had sensed the turbulence in its monastery above. If, in that particular monastery, the monks had been shot on the spot or if they'd had to dance through the town first. If those who'd refused to dance had had the soles of their feet singed with a branding iron, until at last it appeared as if they were dancing. Or had the monks been taken into the forest, away from the resisting townspeople, where only the pines witnessed their transformation: golden crosses torn from necks, rings wrenched off fingers, long hair and beards shaved to render them indistinguishable from the other bodies waiting in the pit graves. I did not want to know any of it, but the questions kept marching into my head until I seized the mummy, pulled it out of the case, and set it on the steel ledge. The body was surprisingly light, as though stuffed with straw. It gave off a sour dust that assailed the back of my throat like a long hairy tongue.

Coughing, sneezing, I attacked the old lightbulb. I pulled, pushed, wriggled, cursed until, at last, my arm shot back with the freed bulb.

I saw it then: the saint teetered on the ledge, tipped toward the floor. I dove to catch it—too late. For such a light object, the crash was momentous, as though the saint had resolutely hurled itself to the ground.

I stared in disbelief as this alleged producer of miracles, the rising star of saints of Ukraine, lay facedown on the floor.

The ledge had been wide enough for the saint—more than wide enough, or I would not have placed the bundle of bones upon it. My exertions with the bulb must have caused the entire counter to shake, and the saint to shimmy toward the edge.

Where the saint's face had made contact with the tiles lay its teeth. Nine of them, nacreous as pearls, roots curved like claws. Without question I would have to glue them back in. The teeth were integral to the saint's reputation, which was integral to me keeping my job.

Carefully, I stowed the saint back inside the display case, my palm beneath its head. The skin under the sparse hair felt leathery, like the rind of a baked ham.

Since I did not have glue, the teeth touch-up would have to wait until evening. Soon the pilgrims would start lining up, clutching coins for admission, and Konstantyn Illych's keys would scratch at the door's many locks. The austere tomb lacked a suitable hiding spot for the teeth—the saint's robes, perhaps, but I could not bring myself to rummage through them—so I slipped the teeth into my pants pocket for the day.

I noticed a few straw-yellow hairs clinging to my palm. I shook my hand, my arm, my entire body, until I was free of them.

Back when I asked Konstantyn Illych for the guard job, he'd inquired if I had experience managing crowds. I assured him

I did. During my time at the agency, I'd even worked with pilgrims. "You mean, worked against," presumed Konstantyn Illych, but neither of us were in the mood to quibble over semantics.

What I meant was that, at the agency, one of my tasks had been to regulate pedestrian traffic to Udobsklad, a fuel and artificial fertilizer storage facility that had once been a monastery. "Regulate" meant "stop"—a tedious task no one else at the agency wanted, so it was dumped on me, a novice at the time. Every spring, small groups of pilgrims would make an illegal procession of 25 kilometers, sneaking through Kirovka, through the forest, to the arched gates of Udobsklad. This they did in spite of the clearly marked signs warning of hazardous material. At the gates, the pilgrims would sing songs, as they had allegedly done for the past six hundred springs. They still considered the storage facility the holy site of some ancient, highly improbable event. The town council had tolerated the procession until we made an embarrassing discovery: among these fanatics figured respectable citizens—two factory directors and a senior lieutenant. Every spring henceforth I had to intercept groups traveling through Kirovka and fine them. One group tried to pass themselves off as a touring choir, another as a foreign delegation; most of the pilgrims, however, were candid about their purpose of travel, and their loyalty to their cause baffled me. At the end of the day I would trudge back to the office, my suit dusty and shoes scuffed, and my colleagues would make me recount all my dealings with the pilgrims while they laughed. Before long it occurred to me that my colleagues were laughing not at the pilgrims but at me, for having to chase after them.

When, after a few years, the Ministry of Labor and Social

Development converted the storage facility into a psychoneurological *internat* and erected a tall iron fence around it, pilgrimage numbers did drop. But the hardiest pilgrims persisted. They set up at the iron gates and, worst of all, drew in orphans to sing with them.

If I issued too few fines, my superior questioned my vigilance; too many fines, and my superior scolded my stale thinking. And still the pilgrims crept back, year after year.

"Who said you could redecorate?" Konstantyn Illych stood at the doorway of the tomb, nodding at the linen sheet over the saint. Konstantyn Illych's hair was uncombed, still ruffled from sleep. The previous year it had turned white in one burst, like a dandelion gone to seed.

"Why not try it for a day?" I suggested. "Divinity needs a bit of mystery."

Konstantyn Illych closed the door behind him. The pilgrims lined up along the glass wall outside were eyeing the sheet, too. Like Konstantyn Illych, they did not look thrilled by its addition.

"Didn't Zaya keep the saint covered, in a pillowcase?" I reminded him. I'd never met the girl, or the pillowcase, but Konstantyn Illych had supplied me with plenty of details.

My superior's scowl softened. "I still have that pillowcase, starched and ironed for her return." His eyes darted about the tomb, as though the girl might materialize at any moment. I suspected that his ex-wife's new living arrangement added to his anguish. He'd once told me that women only turn to each other when there is a dearth of sensible men—"And am I not sensible?"—but I believed the core of his heartbreak lay elsewhere. While Milena had gained two children, who trailed around her in their school pinafores, braids bouncing—he had lost one. Surely he dreamed of walking Zaya to school, no matter her age, her hand clasped in his.

Konstantyn Illych unlocked the cash register and broke a roll of coins into it. He turned back to the shrouded mummy. "Nice not to have to look at that thing," he conceded.

"Or have it look at you," I muttered.

He placed a stack of laundered kerchiefs on his counter, available for rent to women who wished to cover their hair for worship but had forgotten to bring their own—a new addition to his business, following repeated requests.

"So long as the sheet doesn't affect attendance," Konstantyn Illych warned.

At the agency, we'd shared a courtyard with the Transport Workers' Union. One afternoon, on break, I'd overheard two railway engineers debate the best location for a new freight rail yard. The first potential spot sat north of Kirovka and would require the construction of a bridge. The second sat south of Kirovka, over Holinka Ridge, and would require the dynamiting of a tunnel. At the mention of Holinka Ridge, I put down my fish sandwich. The pilgrimage route I'd been monitoring passed over Holinka Ridge. Twenty rows of freight cars would lob off the procession, remove the need for policing any fence. I envisioned myself free from the tedium of chasing down pedestrians, promoted to more rewarding work.

Soon the engineers were yelling at each other, one waving her arms to make herself look larger, the other sitting with arms and legs crossed, unmovable in her granite-gray suit. At last they agreed to flip a coin. If a coin could break the tie between the Soviet Union and Italy in the 1968 European Football Championship, a coin could solve this much simpler matter.

A furious rummaging of pockets ensued.

But no coin!

The engineers turned to the table next to theirs, where I happened to be sitting. Their eyes flitted from my chin, still blotched from a not-unrecent adolescence, to my fish-flake-littered trousers, to the twiggy ankles that stuck out of them. The women's hard faces thawed with pity. I set my jaw. They must not have known who I was or where I worked.

I slid a copper coin from my pocket.

"If you wouldn't mind flipping it for us," said the engineer in the suit, arms still crossed. "We need a neutral arbiter."

"Oh, I couldn't." I was not being bashful—I had never flipped a coin.

A small audience of transport workers gathered around us. I waited for a volunteer to step forward, but none did. The unspoken rule: Your coin, your toss.

"Heads, we build south," said the engineer in the suit.

"Tails, north," deduced the other.

The transport workers cheered me on. Emboldened, I shook the coin between my palms like a die. Heads, heads, I chanted in my mind. I flung my hands out, imagining I were releasing a bird. The coin made a lazy arc over my head, bounced off my shoulder, and landed on the engineers' table, where it rolled on its side, slowly and pathetically, before falling between the wooden slats. A few spectators laughed. Neither of the engineers would deign to stoop for the coin. I did not want to stoop for it either, but soon I was on all fours, crawling under the table as the crowd goaded me on. Blood rushed to my face. The concrete grated my kneecaps. I hated the onlookers but hated myself even more, spineless as usual.

The result: tails.

I'd seen a one-kopek coin countless times before, of course, but now found myself peeved by the look of its squat elaborately serifed number, the folksy ears of wheat encircling it.

As I slowly rose from under the table, coin lodged in my fist, my eyes met the suited engineer's. My expression must have been apologetic: her shoulders dropped almost imperceptibly—she knew that she had lost.

I focused my gaze on a spot above the crowd, a blemish on the tiled wall behind them. The verdict came meekly, my tongue simply testing it out: "Heads."

"Heads," declared the suited engineer, voice hoarse.

"But neither of us saw it," the other engineer pleaded.

"Heads," shouted the crowd, over and over.

"Heads," I shouted with them.

The same hardware sales boy as yesterday intercepted me by the glue section of his tent. "Which type you looking for?"

Hundreds of tubes of all sizes and colors hung before me. I pretended to read their labels, wishing the boy would leave me alone.

He asked, "Permanent or semipermanent?"

He asked, "Food grade?"

He asked, "Medical grade?"

He asked, "Spray-on?"

"Just the standard," I conceded.

He asked, possibly rhetorically, "What *is* standard?" He unhooked a fat horseradish-colored tube, then a pink thimble-size one. "There's the standard glue for wood planks, and the standard glue for the heirloom teapot your wife doesn't know you broke."

"Closer to the latter."

The boy chuckled, conspiratorial, as if he himself had been married for years, had shattered many teapots. "Now," he said in a low voice, "are we talking vitreous porcelain, new Sèvres porcelain, or soft feldspathic porcelain?"

Too many minutes later, on my way back to the tomb, I stopped by a news kiosk for an issue of *Izvestia*. Recently the publication of archives had slowed. Readers were satiated. Back when they knew less, they'd felt safer.

I came upon an article about the rail yard that had been constructed south of Holinka Ridge. I'd almost missed it, wedged as it was between an advertisement for pantyhose and another for tax lawyers. During the rail yard's twelve-year operation, the article informed its readers, the pilgrims who had died crawling under trains in an attempt to reach the monastery numbered:

Men	6
Women	7
Children	2

I hadn't known the true numbers. Shortly after the construction of the rail yard had begun, my superior had declared the pilgrimage issue solved and taken me off the case. I'd ignored the rumors that there had been injuries, even deaths. Now I stared at the neat stack of numbers, reprinted from a railway report. I wondered, uselessly: Why were the children a separate, ungendered category? But as soon as I thought this, my mind conjured them—two girls, then two boys, then a girl and a boy, darting under the maze of freight cars, losing themselves in their game—and I clamped my eyes shut, as if I could unsee them.

If the rail yard had been built instead in the northern spot, zero pilgrims would have died. But the engineer who had vied for the southern rail yard had been the more charismatic, resolved one—surely she would have won, even without a coin toss, even without me skewing the result.

I waited until nightfall to mend the mummy. Inside the tomb, I kept the lights off to avoid attracting attention; a nearby streetlamp provided just enough illumination and, for the finer work, I was armed with a key chain flashlight. Glue at the ready, I reached into my pants pocket for the saint's teeth, but found only a small hole where before there had been none. I searched the other pants pocket, then all four pockets of my coat. My hand returned to the first pocket, to confirm the teeth were still missing.

If the hole had already been there, before the teeth, surely I would have caught it—the pants were my last remaining pair presentable enough for work, and I was vigilant about identifying and repairing any damage—and I would not have used a compromised pocket for valuables. For a moment I entertained the possibility that the teeth had chewed their way out. But no, I told myself, this was simply a case of bad luck, even if I did not believe in luck, bad or good.

I dreaded explaining the saint's disfigurement to Konstantyn Illych. I could not keep it hidden under the linen for much longer—Konstantyn Illych had asked to check on the saint the next morning, and I'd lied and said I'd temporarily misplaced the sole key to the case. If he saw that the teeth were missing, perhaps he'd think I gouged them out, and sold them on the black market. On occasion, relic hunters did visit the tomb. They were easy to spot. They'd kneel the lowest, pray the loudest, before offering money for a tuft of holy hair, a sliver of ear. From their corner-mouth whispers I had learned that five heads of St. John the Baptist were in circulation; thirteen palms, nineteen feet, and twenty-one skull fragments of Jezebel—whatever the dogs didn't eat; the foreskins of Christ and His footprints were particularly popular, as were the moans of David, the shivers of Jehovah.

Just then, between two floor tiles, an incisor twinkled in the lamplight.

I fell to my knees, ready almost to kiss this relic. This time I wrapped the tooth in one of the rental kerchiefs from the counter, and stowed it in my double-lined breast pocket.

Another tooth, longer, fanglike, winked at me by the exit. I collected it, stepped outside. One by one the saint's teeth appeared like stars in a darkening sky.

The third tooth glowed from a crack in the pavement.

The fourth and fifth teeth sat at the rusty foot of a seesaw.

They led me further and further from the tomb. I expected the teeth would retrace the route I'd taken earlier that day from the bazaar, but instead they led me in the opposite direction, toward an unlit park, as though someone had rearranged them as a sinister joke. It was imprudent to be out after sunset, when only thieves and thugs stalked the streets, but I kept on. I tried to imagine myself as a lover, following rose petals to a bed, but couldn't help feeling like a rodent, lured by crumbs to a trap.

The sixth tooth lounged on a tree root.

The seventh spilled from a half-eaten bag of chips.

The eighth bounced between a stray cat's paws.

I stopped there. I'd reached the perimeter of the park. Its patchy lawn sloped down to a copse of oaks and a well that had run dry. I needed that last tooth, but was afraid of where it might appear—at the bottom of the well? Under a sleeping pack of dogs? I inhaled the cool night air, tried to compose myself. These were only teeth, after all; I'd been living with a set of my own for forty years. I set off at a trot, down a paved path. When I spotted the ninth tooth roosting in an old flower bed under the oaks, lucent as its siblings, the tightness in my chest broke into laughter. Was this where the teeth had been leading me? To a patch of weeds? Carried by a senseless impulse to catch the tooth before it got away, I lunged forward. My foot caught a notch in the pavement. As I hurled to the ground, my screaming jaws bit into the concrete rim of the flower bed.

I do not know how long I lay in the dark, swallowing blood.

My heart climbed into my head and pounded at my eardrums, seeking escape. My jaws ground at the hinges. I spat out what I hoped was gravel. I clutched the saint's last tooth. Its claw sank into my palm.

By the time I stumbled back to the tomb, my entire body felt seared with pain. When I turned on the bathroom light, a bloated, scratched face stared at me from the mirror. A criminal's face. The lips oozed blood. I willed the mouth to open, but now my jaws were stuck shut. This was partly a relief—I did not want to see the damage my tongue had already rooted out. Rotten from a lifetime of avoiding stomatologists, my front teeth had given way easily. Their absence felt vertiginous. My tongue kept back, as though it, too, were in danger of tumbling out, and pressed itself against the molars. A few of these were fractured, their edges jutting sharply.

I opened the saint's display case, yanked off the linen sheet. Now the saint's crinkled eyes and thrown-open mouth seemed to be laughing. I knew then where the teeth had been leading me: not just to the flower bed, but also to the notch in the pavement.

I uncapped the tube of glue. Its cloying smell spiked my headache, brought on a wave of nausea. I reached into my breast pocket, unwrapped the kerchief. Inside, I found only a hole. With increasing horror, I discovered that the pocket, too, had a new hole. This time I could not chalk up the loss to bad luck: the teeth had gnawed through both layers of lining. And yet again they were at large, free to wreak havoc upon me.

When a locomotive begins to pull its train, the couplers between the cars tighten with a clack. The clack skips all the way down the train, head to tail, like the cracking of a spine.

When a locomotive begins to pull its train, and a person happens to be crawling under it, they hear the clacks pass over them. A warning: *get out, get out, get out.* Yet these pilgrims, these men, women, children, had crept on. In their final moments, did they regret what they were doing? Did they still believe that something better waited on the other side?

"Are you in trouble?" Konstantyn Illych asked me the following morning. "I don't want trouble in my tomb."

It was fifteen minutes before opening. I tried to ignore the many pairs of eyes trained on me through the glass wall. The swelling of my face and hands had grown overnight. A magenta bruise extended from the corners of my scabbed lips, giving me a clown's smile. My gums still leaked blood. Konstantyn Illych did not seem to believe a flower bed could do this much damage.

I couldn't bring myself to tell Konstantyn Illych the truth: yes, I was in trouble, just not the kind of trouble he meant. "I told you. I tripped," I mumbled. I still could not open my mouth more than a few millimeters.

A freckled teenage boy knocked on one of the glass panes, trying to catch my attention.

"If Zaya comes back and I'm not here, she'll see your face and run again," said Konstantyn Illych.

"I'll run after her."

"You haven't seen her run." He gazed at me as if we were separated by a great gulf; he had someone to love and I didn't.

"You never told me where Zaya got the saint." By now I had a hunch, and I dreaded the answer.

Konstantyn Illych scowled, pretending not to understand my muffled speech. I repeated the question, and he shrugged. "Her orphanage."

"You mean that former monastery?"

He glanced at the pilgrims. "Keep those pretty lips sealed. I hear the Church is trying to reappropriate what it can."

I began to shiver, and longed to run from the tomb, into the warm sunlight.

Konstantyn Illych slapped my shoulder affectionately. The muscles at the back of my neck locked in spasm. "You can take the day off, but I can't promise to pay you for it." He urged me to go see a stomatologist, but we both knew this was impossible. The last public clinic in town had closed, and few could afford the glittering private one.

I stayed in the tomb. We opened on time.

—

The duty of a guard is to be still, to be present with the world. But over the next several days I could not keep still. Every cell in my body howled. The bruising and swelling began to subside, but the pain did not. Its hooks jerked at my gums, at the exposed nerves of my shattered teeth. I subsisted on potato broth and sour cream, and my stomach wrung itself with hunger.

When I wasn't thinking of my teeth, I thought of the saint's. I feared their reappearance, their reassembly. I feared they would punish me, as the noose had punished my ex-colleague. The teeth would gnash me to bits. There were moments when, as if on cue, a pilgrim would turn toward me and I'd catch an opaline glint. In the evenings, I shook out my slippers, felt under my pillow. I even peeked under the saint's shroud, hoping the teeth had tired of their wanderings and resumed their post. But the saint remained as gap-mouthed as a child.

Each shift stretched longer and longer. My fingers fidgeted with the hole in my pants pocket, worrying it larger. I counted and re-counted the pilgrims. Counting was not part of the job. I did not like the crowd, and quantifying it made it seem even larger, but I couldn't help myself. I counted the men in sixes. The women in sevens. The children in twos. I imagined them crawling. Flat on the ground.

Thanks to the linen sheet, the relic hunter whispered in my ear, no one would know if they were appealing to a saint or a pile of sandbags. And wasn't that the power of prayer? The woman brought her taper candle closer to her face, the light from its flame stretching shadows across her features. She kept on: If a saint, no, half a saint, brought this much hope, imagine what would happen if that saint were divided further, into many pieces, displayed in many glass boxes across many churches and homes. Didn't I want to maximize hope? She offered me a fine price. Would even throw in the sandbags.

It was a Sunday evening, which was when Konstantyn Illych habitually kept the tomb illuminated with sixty candles for sixty minutes. The weekly vigil coincided with the blackouts, which had started up again for the first time in years, but only in small towns like ours.

From her purse the relic hunter slid a yellowed portrait of a boy posing with a poodle. She positioned it among the other photographs on the display case. Likely she'd bought her prop at a flea market, to help her impersonate a pilgrim. The relationship was almost believable: the relic hunter and the boy in the photo shared pointed, elfish ears.

By the cash register, Konstantyn Illych's head craned over the crowd. His gaze landed on us. He shook his head at me in sympathy. They can be so *chatty*, he seemed to say. So *whiny*.

"That boy is someone's son," I whispered to the hunter.

"He was my sister's." Her dark eyes met mine, daring me to utter another rebuke. "Do we have a deal?"

For a second I considered; I desperately needed the money, and it would have pleased me to be rid of the mummy. But selling it to a butcher's block felt like a renewed violence. The duty of a guard is to guard, not to steal, and especially not from Konstantyn Illych. He had given me the job out of goodwill and I could not betray him. I shook my head.

—

I decided my pain was a test of will. To distract my thoughts from my mouth, and my stomach—I still couldn't chew solids—I instituted a Changing of the Guard. If we wanted to build a world-class tomb, I told Konstantyn Illych, we needed the pageantry.

Two minutes and forty-five seconds before the hour, every hour, I held the line. I marched out to the front of 1933 Ivansk, high-kicking Prussian style, upper body stiff while my lower body danced away the pressure that had accumulated during the past fifty-seven minutes and fifteen seconds. The old guard charged around the building. Precisely as the clock struck the hour, the new guard marched in from the opposite side. On occasion a child might call out, "But isn't that the same man as before?" and a snigger would ripple through the crowd. But I paid no heed. My choreography grew more and more elaborate: all taps, skips, and kicks, a wild whir of legs, as though the earth singed my feet.

Konstantyn Illych encouraged my displays; they were drawing larger crowds, which assembled at the top of the hour to cheer on my footwork. By the end of every shift I would exhaust myself, wanting nothing more than the sweet numbness of sleep. After two weeks, however, my hunger gave way to weakness. I lived with a sharp ringing in my skull, the air having condensed into two drills that bore into my ears. My uniform hung from my thinning limbs. I stumbled through the Changing of the Guard, then reduced its frequency, then gave it up. After that, I simply kept to my post, where the pain awaited me hotly, with pincers for arms and clamps for lips.

—

A knock on the glass wall startled me awake. The streetlamp illuminated the silhouette of a great hairy beast. It watched me for some time before peeling back the fur from its head. I recognized the naked ears that stuck out.

I heaved myself from my cot and waited out a spell of dizziness before shuffling to the door. I unlocked the dead bolt and cracked open the door, its chain still hinged.

The relic hunter's floor-length coat rippled in the orange lamplight. "Name your price."

I'd once heard a pensioner lament that to get your teeth fixed you had to give up a kidney. Without expecting an answer, I asked the hunter how much a kidney cost.

Without a blink she said, "Thirty-five thousand." She peered at my face. "Why, finally getting those teeth done? For thirty-five thousand, you'll be good as new." She thrust her hand through the door crack. "Final offer."

I cringed at the thought of the saint hacked to pieces. But the saint was already dead, as were the men, women, and children who crawled behind my eyes day and night. And here I was, living.

I gripped the relic hunter's hand. I wanted that hand, warm and moist, to pull me from the tomb, from my wrecked body.

Victims, the newspaper article had called the perished pilgrims. (The railway report itself had not called them anything, only quantified them.) When dredging up the past, the newspapers attempted to divide its players into victims and villains. My employment at the agency would mark me as the latter. But I had suffered, too. I'd grown up without parents. If a coin flip hadn't decided their fate, likely the tick of a pen had, or an act similarly arbitrary. After three generations, who were the victims, who the villains? We'd become a formidable alloy, bound by shame. The grand dream of equality realized.

I'd braced myself for the stomatological clinic of my childhood: a warehouse with many rows of barbershop chairs, in which a patient endured not only his or her own (unanesthetized) agony, but that of the other wailing patients.

But here, in the reception room of the new private clinic, a burbling fountain induced calm. Glossy posters attested to miraculous Before-and-Afters. Anything could be erased: nicotine and caffeine stains, calculus so thick it could be mined, maxillofacial birth defects, industrial accidents, head-on collisions.

After I laid out the stacks of bills on the counter, a rosy-cheeked stomatologist led me down a corridor. She lifted her chin and thrust back her broad shoulders with the bravado of an opera singer about to step onto the stage. Then she opened a door to a private sunlit room. A mint-green reclining chair greeted me, curved arms inviting, as though it had been waiting for me all along. The instruments of torture were nowhere in sight.

As she inspected my mouth, the stomatologist made small sounds of anguish. "Poor sir," she murmured, "poor sir." I lapped up the words; I hadn't realized how badly I needed them.

"For a case as severe as yours," the stomatologist pronounced, "only Western technology will do." She would extract my remaining teeth, which were past their prime anyway, drill holes directly into my jawbone, screw in implants with titanium rods. I recoiled at the idea, but already she had pressed a button, and the chair reclined until my head felt lower than my feet. My face had lost all color, she reported. She worried I would faint.

"The pain," I asked, "will it go away?"

The stomatologist waved away the question—it seemed beside the point. I would have the best smile in town, she assured me. She hooked a surgical mask over her ears.

It was not until she latched the anesthesia mask over my nose and instructed me to count down from ten that the instruments scurried from their hiding places. With a hydraulic wheeze, a metal tray rose from behind the chair, containing an assortment of pliers. Then came another tray, with two sparkling rows of drill heads. An oval lamp hovered over my face. I felt myself to be on the belly of a spider, each leg performing a task. The final metal dish slid into view, containing the implants. Panic seized me—I recognized their nacreous gleam.

The saint's teeth grinned at me from the dish, the full set, their roots now titanium.

I tried to warn the stomatologist about the cursed teeth, but my tongue refused to stir, my lips flapped uselessly. The room contracted around the stomatologist's blue eyes. They crinkled. Under her mask, she must have been smiling. My fear spiked, then burned away. All I could do was accept what was coming, like the clacks of a train pulled into motion. "You aren't counting, Mikhail Ivanovich. Start counting down."

ROACH BROOCH

Those who mourn quietest, mourn deepest.

When the grandson dies, the rest of the family squabbles over his estate, but the grandparents vow not to get involved. (Not all the grandparents—just the maternal set, Pyotr Palashkin and Lila Palashkina, the last of the family to live in glum little Kirovka, while the rest have escaped.) Considering the shedload of money the grandson earned abroad, doing who knows what, he must have written a will, as people abroad do. The grandparents think: The rest of the family will surely respect his wishes.

When the grandson's parents inherit his apartment and car, Pyotr and Lila don't grumble that these parents already own a two-room and don't drive.

When the grandson's girlfriend inherits the diamond ring he kept in his lockbox, it would be rude to remind her that he hadn't proposed yet, might've changed his mind.

The grandparents don't mention that they practically raised the grandson while his parents worked. He was the first grandchild, the only one they could help care for before the family dispersed. The child was born joyless, and they would try and try to cheer him up by pointing out small miracles: the first crocus bursting through snow; the newspaper photo of the crocodile who wears his turtle friend as a hat; the eerie curling of one's fingers when the inner wrist is pressed. If the grandparents couldn't make the boy happy, at least they kept him clean, fed—alive.

Everyone in the family is poor, but the grandparents are the poorest. When the Union fell and inflation spiked, their lifelong savings dissolved along with their peaceful retirement. Instead of lounging on his bench in front of 1933 Ivansk—the bench now swallowed by a sea of pilgrims—Pyotr sits with Lila on a pair of children's foldout chairs at the train station, selling bone albums to tourists on layover. They greet the tourists in a dim underpass that reeks of urine, the bone records spread over a checkered tablecloth on the concrete. Other elderly citizens sell Soviet army regalia, reprinted propaganda posters, painted wooden spoons. To procure the X-rays, the grandparents have to dig through the dumpsters behind the polyclinic, risking infection and grisly new diseases. Pyotr and Lila got into the business when a neighbor, Milena Markivna, posted an ad in the lobby offering her bone music equipment for a reasonable price. Included were a modified gramophone and sixteen vinyl records. The grandparents were overwhelmed with joy the first time they held the albums: Red Poppies! Jolly Fellows! Such ensembles used to perform on television all the time, with their smart suits or matching knit sweaters, bobbing in sync, abstaining from flashy dance. Pyotr and Lila couldn't hide their disappointment when Milena told them the vinyl sleeves and labels had been a disguise, that the *real* music only came through when you lowered the needle.

The record player turned out to be in poor condition, likely kept in the damp for years, and the volume knob broke at first touch. It's still stuck to one level: blaring. The grandparents have to live with Alice Cooper, KISS, Black Sabbath at full growl. It wouldn't be so bad if they couldn't understand the words, but Pyotr and Lila are retired English teachers.

"GO TO HELL," the music advises. "LIE DOWN AND DIE."

Also, "YOU SHOULD HAVE NEVER HAPPENED."

But, of small comfort: "I'LL MISS YOU WHEN YOU'RE GONE."

The family doesn't think the situation is so bad. After all, the grandparents get to listen to music all day, and make money doing it. Meanwhile the others have to drive trucks across the country, bend over microscopes at catheter assembly lines, check fares on packed trams, hawk bread out of moving trains. And those are just the day jobs.

"Grandfather has a tumor," Lila likes to remind the family over the phone, whenever they get smug. The tumor sits atop his bladder.

"Benign," they snap back.

"But growing, crowding out his organs," she tells them. "Even if very slowly, it will kill him."

"So get it removed!" The family has been pleading for this to happen for years.

But the situation isn't as simple as that. The grandparents can't get the tumor removed because as long as it exists, they're guaranteed a monthly pelvic X-ray. The shape of the spine and hips in the X-ray reminds the tourists of an electric guitar, and they snap that bone album up right away. The tumor is what feeds the grandparents.

"Why not just make copies of the same X-ray?" This, the snarky uncle.

"Don't think we haven't tried," Lila says. But no one in town will make copies. They've even asked the polyclinic receptionist for extras, and the woman in turn asked what they thought she was running, a medical facility or an X-ray press.

Finally the relatives sort out what the grandparents will inherit. Something the grandson must have treasured very much, they promise. They send one of the teenagers over to deliver it. A head taller than the last time the grandparents saw him, and newly handsome, the teenager carries a clear-lidded tin box repurposed from Belgian chocolates. With his stiff posture, bearing the gift in his arms, he looks like a suitor. He won't come inside, though, says he has to rush off to catch the next train back to his city, a train that doesn't stop here anymore, not fully—it only slows to a crawl along the platform because the town no longer deserves more than a minute of the train's time.

Since the major items have already been allotted, the grandparents aren't expecting an enormous or life-changing gift. They'd be happy with a keepsake, however small.

The tin box in the teenager's hands has a pinprick hole. Lila takes the box and peers into it, her mouth already set in a smile.

Inside the box is, well, the grandparents aren't sure what. A silver chain attached to an oblong pile of brown rocks, sitting on a piece of newspaper. It's roughly the size and shape of a stool. It looks much like the samples the grandson had to produce in his childhood, to be scooped into a matchbox—by the grandmother, who else?—then wrapped in newspaper, then a plastic bag, and submitted to the school nurse, who inspected it for worms. Each looming inspection would make the boy nervous, thus constipated—stage fright, Pyotr called it—and Lila would often have to produce the sample herself. The rest of the family liked to joke that the grandson would one day return the favor.

Is that what the so-called gift is about?

The most disgusting thing about the brown pile: two hairs sticking out of one end.

The grandparents look up from the box, but the teenager has already run off.

The pair of hairs twitches.

In shock, Lila almost drops the box. Now the entire pile lumbers from one side of the box to the other, toward its own reflection.

The grandparents draw their faces closer. The rocks, they realize, are glued to an insect. A giant wingless roach, by the looks of it. The hairs are its antennae.

Is it supposed to be a pet?

An art project?

Just the kind of thing the grandson would waste his money on.

The rest of the family may not know it yet, but Pyotr and Lila have stopped talking to them. If one of the relatives were to call, the grandparents wouldn't answer.

The grandparents keep up with the bone records. Keep ignoring the doctor's pleas to remove the tumor. The doctor brings props to the radiology room each month, to demonstrate the tumor's growth.

He holds up a pea. "Where we started."

He holds up a glossy chestnut. "Where we're at."

He holds up a lemon. "Where we'll be in a few short years."

Not the regular type of lemon, pale and pitted, Lila notes. This one is dark yellow, taut-bellied. Likely a Meyer, from a pricey store.

"Am I getting through?" the doctor asks. He's taut-bellied himself, with brown nicotine stains on his lips.

The grandparents nod along, but the gravity of the diagnosis has never quite sunk in. It just doesn't make sense, how a pea can metamorphose into a chestnut, then a lemon.

"Can we keep the lemon?" Pyotr asks.

At their sales stall, the grandparents keep a pair of flashlights. Tourists shine them through the X-ray records. Sometimes the reason for the X-ray is obvious: a broken limb, a spoon floating in a stomach. Other times, the X-ray shows a subtle swelling, a hairline fracture. The tourists enjoy the detective work.

For the layperson, Pyotr's tumor isn't easy to identify. Lila has to trace the faint orb above the bladder with her finger before the tourists say "Ah." She never attributes the tumor to her husband, sitting right beside her, so as not to dampen anyone's mood.

As with any growth or deformity, the tourists always want to know: "A victim of . . . ?" The tourists don't want to say the dirty word themselves, but are itching to hear it, pronounced authentically by this kerchiefed babushka.

Lila casts down her eyes, confirms: "Chernobyl."

She says this even though her husband never served in Chernobyl or had anything to do with it. The most he'd done was help hose off their apartment building, as per government recommendations, but the spray of the garden hose only reached the second floor, and they lived on the third, so who knew how much of the fallout they'd absorbed? The government had also recommended they drink wine to protect against the radiation, but the grandparents didn't have wine themselves and didn't know anyone so fancy. Pyotr's skin hadn't melted off like that poor woman's had, the one on the local news—she'd bathed in one of the rivers—but no one can prove that he *isn't* a victim. And the people who might take issue with the misuse of the term, the ones most territorial about it, tend to be dead.

Anyway, at the word "Chernobyl," the tourists have their wallets out.

The grandparents are eating nettle soup when they spot the roach sitting right above them, on the kitchen ceiling. Its silver chain swings back and forth as though to hypnotize them. Pyotr drops his spoon into his soup.

The lid of the tin box must have come open when Lila shoved it into the closet. But she doesn't want to be the one to put the roach back in the box.

Pyotr won't put it back either, even though pests are his domain, his only domain, while Lila cooks, cleans, and all the rest.

The roach stays on the ceiling, and the grandparents endure their meal.

They make sure not to leave any food out, hoping that the thing will leave the apartment on its own. But in the coming weeks, every time they think it's finally gone, it skulks out from under the stove or shoe rack, from between their clothes in the wardrobe, the chain dragging behind it.

—

What if something were to happen to the grandparents? Say they were to perish in a fire. Just last month, a sickeningly sweet smoke rose through the vents from one of the suites below, pouring into theirs, and Lila threw her best linens from the balcony to save them. Or the grandparents might succumb to gas poisoning. At this very moment, they could be two blue corpses splayed out on the floor—and the rest of the family wouldn't know it.

These past few weeks, no one has checked in.

Or maybe the family has tried to check in but the grandparents couldn't hear the phone ring over the roaring music.

"YOU'RE A TENDER LILY," the record player shrieks, "STUCK TO THE BOTTOM OF MY BOOT."

Maybe the family tried sending a letter, but the new mailman can't find the grandparents' building because some idiot chiseled the numbers out of the concrete beside the entrance all those years ago. Pyotr borrows a pink piece of chalk from the children hopscotching on the road, braves the crowd of pilgrims at the front of the building, and writes a large blocky "1933" above where the stenciled numbers used to be.

The family may even have tried to visit, but didn't knock loudly enough. Lila posts a note on the door: KNOCK LOUDLY. The grandmother's own grandmother had a sign like that on her gate in the village: KNOCK HARD OR THROW A ROCK AT THE DOG. At least she had a dog. All the grandparents have is this oversize roach.

And don't any of their children have a spare key? Maybe Lila should mail one of the daughters a spare key—just a key, no note or any other sign of life.

"Maybe we should just call everyone," Pyotr suggests. "Make sure they haven't been trying to check on us."

"Then what? They'll hear from us and won't need to check on us."

By having all these children, Pyotr and Lila thought they'd buffered themselves against isolation. Instead, the grandparents don't have friends because of all the time they put into the children. First came the sons, which Pyotr and Lila kept having until, finally, came the daughters. Daughters are supposed to stick around, help out. But now all the daughters live just as far away as the sons, in big cities with job prospects, busy caring for their own children, believing those children will stick around.

Maybe it's a law of physics. Once a baby is expelled, it will keep moving away at a constant speed unless acted upon.

Not that the grandparents will act first.

To repurpose the tin box, Lila yanks out the newspaper lining. Under the lining she discovers a glossy pamphlet featuring a photo of a fine-boned man in a plum blazer. Tethered to his lapel is a rock-laden insect just like the one the grandparents received. It emits a dull sheen, like a dusty brooch. Lila can't understand why anyone would wear a cockroach.

The Madagascar hissing cockroach, the manual explains. They breed under rotting jungle logs. The embellishments on their carapaces are among the rarest gems in the world: serendibite, in its uncut form.

"Serendibite," Lila repeats.

Rarer than diamonds, the manual insists. Infinitely more valuable. And on your pet, priceless.

—

When was the last time the grandparents saw the roach? Last week? Last month? They're ready to tear the whole apartment apart.

"The last piece of our grandson," Lila laments.

"His most beloved pet," says Pyotr. "And we lost it."

They find it two minutes later, drinking from a leaky valve under the kitchen sink. Lila plucks the roach off by the chain and it pirouettes in the air. In the strong midday light, its gems give off a bronze glint. The grandparents marvel at them.

When Lila lowers the insect into its tin box, Pyotr asks, "What now?"

"We care for it like we cared for our grandson," says Lila. Unpleasant as the grandson was as a child—with his mercurial stomach, his bulge-eyed tantrums—they never gave up.

The Madagascar hissing cockroach makes the easiest pet, the manual assures the grandparents. The Madagascar hissing cockroach is perfectly content with the simplest foods, like carrots! But it always loves a taste of home: guavas and papayas, lightly rotten.

The grandparents don't know what guavas and papayas look like, so assume they are expensive.

Provide plenty of water, to be replaced daily, the manual instructs. To mitigate the risk of drowning, place a sponge in the bowl, to be replaced weekly.

The grandparents don't use sponges themselves, only rags from old underwear.

The Madagascar hissing cockroach does not like direct sun-light, the manual warns. Wear the roach brooch only at night, otherwise your pet will burrow down your collar or into your hair.

Oh, and the Madagascar hissing cockroach is very clean, cleaner than people, but if kept under less-than-ideal condi-tions it is known to harbor up to fourteen species of mold, some of which are potent allergens. In the event of a mold outbreak, simply place the roach into a plastic bag with a half cup of extra-fine flour, gently shake the bag to dislodge the fungal roots— you may even have to rub the roach a little—transfer the roach to a sieve deep enough to prevent escape, and repeat as many times as needed to remove all the mold. Don't forget to vacuum the carpets, linen, and furniture to get any straggling spores, run an air purifier/dehumidifier, throw all your clothes into the laundry, and, finally, scrub your hair and skin. Reevaluate why you had the outbreak in the first place, and find ways to improve your cleanliness.

What the grandparents reevaluate: the grandson's wishes. What he truly wanted for them wasn't a pet cockroach, but a better life, a peaceful retirement. He would have wanted them to give up the bone record business, get that tumor removed. Turn that dreadful music off.

The pawnshop owner, a hulking man in a squeaky leather jacket, won't touch the roach brooch.

"Roach brooches are the rage in the highest fashion circles,"

Lila insists. She shows him the photograph of the model wearing a roach, but the pawnshop owner doesn't seem to know about these fashion circles.

"The gems are among the rarest in the world," says Pyotr. "Serendibite."

The pawnshop owner laughs, as if Pyotr has made up a word.

Later that week in the train station underpass, the grandparents try to sell the roach brooch to a French tourist, a rich-looking one. The woman has a mink fur coiled around her neck, the animal's tiny jaws clasped to its own rear. Lila tells the tourist that this is one of those mutant Chernobyl cockroaches, the ones there are rumors about.

"But why glue rocks onto it?" the French tourist asks.

"Serendibite," Pyotr shouts.

At last the grandparents find a jeweler two towns over, an ancient man whose skin hangs from his face and arms in doughy sheets. When he opens the box to appraise the contents, the roach gives a loud hiss, like an old bus when its brake is released, and scrambles up the jeweler's sleeve. The jeweler screams, slaps his arm, then elbow and shoulder, as though to put out a fire. He stops screaming only when he frees himself from his shirt and locks himself in the bathroom. It takes Pyotr and Lila half an hour to coax the roach from under the cabinet using crumbs and lint from their pockets.

"So long as the gems are touching that thing," the jeweler declares behind the bathroom door, "I'm not touching the gems."

—

Never attempt to remove the gems from the insect, the manual warns. Madagascar hissing cockroaches have a natural waxy covering, and the patented technology used to attach the gems took months to develop. They won't come off without harm to your pet.

Of course, the grandparents don't want to do harm.

Even in the labor camps, the guards would wait until a prisoner died before gouging out a golden tooth—or so Pyotr and Lila read. The rules of civility hold.

Roaches don't live very long anyway. In the past, whenever the apartment had an infestation of the lowly local ones, their corpses soon turned up everywhere.

The best thing about the Madagascar hissing cockroach, the manual proclaims: it can live up to five *years*!

If the grandparents stop putting carrot peels in the roach's box, or refilling the water, it isn't on purpose. They can be so forgetful, with their busy days, with the tumor, with the music that drowns out the tinny scratches coming from the box.

"I'LL BE THERE FOR YOU," the music promises, "WHEN THE FLAMES GET HIGHER."

The scratches may cease any day now.

Which family member will call first? One of the daughters, surely. But which?

Whichever daughter calls first will get a share of the money from the serendibite. Of course, this will be a surprise. Pyotr and Lila wouldn't want the money to be the main draw. They witnessed the greedy frenzy after the grandson died, and wouldn't want to repeat it.

Maybe nature isn't a circle of life, but a circle of abandonment.

It's true what they say about roaches surviving anything. Even without food or water, this one is looking as if it will survive both the grandparents.

The grandparents can't bring themselves to smash the roach with a frying pan. They can't fathom killing the last remnant of their grandson so violently, or risk damaging the jewels.

They can't bring themselves to drown it either. Or freeze it. Or suffocate it in a plastic bag.

The only sensible way to deal with it: treat the roach brooch like the insect that it is, and spray it with insecticide.

In a spray bottle, Lila mixes baking soda, chili pepper, soapsuds, and sunflower seed oil (this last one, to block breathing pores).

She turns to her husband. "I cooked, you serve."

Pyotr, solemn, sits the tin box on the kitchen table. He pops the lid with one hand, holds the spray bottle with the other. His finger on the trigger, he wishes the cockroach would try to run, display instinctual fear and distrust, like every other living thing. But the insect sits on its newspaper bed, wiggling its antennae. How could such a gentle creature possibly survive in the jungle?

In the corridor, the phone rings.

The grandparents look at each other in relief.

It must be one of their children. How silly the grandparents have been, to think themselves abandoned. How awful to imagine their beloved daughter (or granddaughter!) waiting at the other end of the line, worrying.

Pyotr stays with the roach while Lila hurries down the corridor. She cradles the phone against her cheek.

A deep male voice fills the line. A stranger's. "Have you taken the jewels off the roach yet?"

Lila's face contorts. She wants to slam the phone down, free the line for the children's calls.

The man introduces himself as an employee of the pawnshop the grandparents visited two weeks ago. Good thing his boss jotted down their phone number, the man says, if only to make them go away.

Lila finds her voice again. "We're just about to take the jewels off."

"Don't." Unlike his boss, this man knows about roach brooches, has seen the catalogs. He's willing to offer a fine price for it. He just needs her to check one tiny thing.

"I'll do anything," Lila says.

"On the roach's belly, between the front and middle sets of legs, should be a tiny RB. Like a logo plaque inside a Prada bag, proving authenticity."

From the corridor, Lila yells the instructions to her husband in the kitchen.

"I can't see its underside," her husband says.

"Lift it up and take a peek," she shouts.

"With my hands?"

"With your hands."

Pyotr holds his breath, hooks his fingers around the carapace. The bits that aren't encrusted with jewels feel slippery, like polished wood. The heft is surprising, and he wonders how much of the weight belongs to the living part of the brooch. The roach's legs swivel wildly as he turns it upside down. Its abdomen is composed of tawny segments that slide in and out of each other. He spots the small black head, bowed like a penitent's, the two matte bumps for eyes.

"I don't see any mark," says Pyotr, staring at the belly.

"My husband is still looking," Lila relays to the pawnbroker.

"It isn't here," says Pyotr.

"It got rubbed off," relays Lila.

"A genuine mark can't get rubbed off. It's branded onto the exoskeleton," the pawnbroker explains. "What you have there is counterfeit, the so-called jewels worthless as pebbles."

"But the insect—that part is real."

"Without the jewels," the pawnbroker says, "it's just a roach."

In the kitchen, Pyotr is still holding the insect. He's entranced by its rear end. There's something wrong with it. A wet white glob is squeezing out. The roach slips from between his fingers and falls onto Pyotr's stomach, where it clings to his woolly sweater. Its weight feels both repulsive and comforting. The white mass begins to separate into wiggling fingers, with tiny black dots at the tips. Eyes. The shimmering nymphs are attached to a string, like a crystal garland. Impossible to count them all as they unspool. Fifty, sixty?

Pyotr has never seen anything like it. His own children were born behind closed doors; he had to wait in a hospital corridor with the other expectant fathers, trying to distinguish his wife's howls from the chorus of other women.

In the light, the babies spring awake, detach themselves from their string. But they don't just scamper away. They crawl all over the mother, and she becomes furry with antennae. They eat the string that once bound them together. This is how they'll grow strong. Within an hour, their shells will harden to a caramel color.

At this very moment, the pawnbroker is imploring Lila to get rid of the knockoff as soon as possible. In the factories, the breeders don't bother to sort the males from the females; often the females are pregnant when sold.

But by the time the grandmother hangs up and reenters the kitchen, the grandfather's sweater is covered with babies. They eat the crumbs from his breakfast, hardly larger than crumbs themselves. Pyotr looks up at Lila and smiles, eyes shining. She can't help but smile with him when he says, "Aren't they beautiful?"

THE ERMINE COAT

On the way back from the bazaar, Aunt Milena points to the cracks under the balconies of our building. She warns me never to walk or stand under them, unlike those pilgrims lined up for the tomb. "Little by little," she says, "we're sinking into the soft earth."

Knowing what comes next, I lift my net sack to my chest, hide behind the leafy beet stalks. Over the past month Aunt Milena has used any excuse to remind me that our family's misfortune is my fault. Even the rat-size cockroach she was trapped with in the elevator last week—also, apparently, my doing. If it weren't for my misbehavior, my mother, sister, and I could have left this collapsing building, this collapsing country.

But Aunt Milena must be feeling generous today. Instead of scolding me, she sits on her haunches, studies her own boot print in the mud. "There used to be a village here," she says, and I imagine one no larger than her foot. She tells me the villagers spoke Ukrainian and picked cranberries for a living. Then the marshes were drained, sunflowers sown for oil, the villagers pried from their dung huts and stacked on top of each other. Many of them refused to move into the high-rises, never having lived so far from the earth. "The village was called Ivankiv," she says. "It lives on as our street name, but Russified." When she lived in the countryside, doing farmwork in exchange for a bed, the villagers would pass down secret lore.

Aunt Milena moved in with us two years ago, after Grandmother died. All she'd brought with her: the clothes on her back, a rapier, a record player and phonograph, and sixteen vinyl records for Mother to sell (but Mother refused, saying the records wouldn't be worth much these days anyway).

Some mornings I find Mother and Aunt Milena twisted around each other on the foldout, mouths agape, as though they escaped the same nightmare, just barely.

Like Mother, Aunt Milena is tall with a long pale face. She and Mother could be sisters. When they drop me and my sister off at school, no one asks, and we don't tell. The neighbors might whisper, but what can they do? Mother says we're living in an age of freedom. Aunt Milena says we're living in an age of fifteen brands of sausage, which is not the same thing as freedom. When I ask where are these fifteen brands of sausage, Mother says we need only visit Kiev to find them. Aunt Milena says no Kirovkavite can afford such an indulgence. But whatever the argument, Aunt Milena never wins, because when Mother takes Aunt Milena's face in her hands and beams her brightest smile, Aunt Milena breaks every time.

Last year, for a five-month stint, Mother and Aunt Milena sewed fur coats for the black market. Mother was already a master seamstress, and Aunt Milena caught on quickly. A large sweaty man whose face hung slack like a bulldog's would come for the coats on Mondays. Volkov never wore fur himself, only velvet tracksuits, usually maroon. After inspecting the coats, he'd toss stacks of *kupony* to Mother and Aunt Milena. Twenty, thirty stacks a week. The new currency looked like play money, with its picture of the Sofia Cathedral getting sucked into a flower-shaped black hole, and Aunt Milena told me it was worth about as much. Volkov would drop the next batch of pelts onto the kitchen table. Always the same slick black pelts, as if Volkov had ripped out the stitching from the week before and returned the pieces to be resewn, over and over. No one knew what type of animal they'd belonged to. Something long, caged. Its thick hairs snuck between our bedsheets, under our eyelids and tongues. I worried I'd start coughing up slimy ropes, as our neighbor's cat was known to do. We picked at our limbs, scratched our scalps. My schoolmates told the nurse I had lice, and if not lice, then definitely worms.

My little sister, five years old, thought everything sold on the black market had to be black. She liked to sit under the kitchen table, tracing the velvet humps of Volkov's calves until Mother yanked her hand away. I wanted his soft thick thighs, to bite through the fat and meat until my teeth hit bone. He'd been rounding out, a sign that his business was steady.

Now, because of me, Mother is back at her old job at a chemical plant two towns over, rumored to be shutting down anytime, and Aunt Milena cleans floors at a lamp factory. They get paid in perfumes and lamps, but the managers promise money soon. Lamps are bad for barter on account of the blackouts, but sometimes our right-side neighbor trades balcony-grown beans for the perfume. From his yowls and moans across the thin walls, we know he drinks it, but I like to think he's taken a lover and the perfume is for her.

As for the left-side neighbor, he gets paid in cosmetics, and Mother says his daughters whore around.

It was a Monday visit from Volkov, six months ago, that sealed our fate. He laid a bundle of parchment paper on the kitchen table, slowly unwrapped it. The furs inside glowed white, making everything else look tired and dirty. Each pelt began with two angry slits, the eyes, and ended with a black-tipped tail.

"Ermine," Volkov said. "Turns white in the winter, except for the tail."

"Why not the tail?" Mother asked.

"Must be how the animals find each other in the snow," Aunt Milena said. "Tiny flags."

"It's how hunters find them," he said.

My sister reached out to stroke a tail but Volkov shook his head, as though worried the furs would wake.

"Royal furs were made from ermine," he said. More impressive still: "Marilyn Monroe wore ermine."

We didn't know what to do with such narrow pieces. Aunt Milena nailed them to wooden boards for stretching, but they seized up, as though panicked. I dug my fingers into the smalls of their backs, the spot that makes the most skittish dog melt. Nothing worked. I understood: the thought of being sewn to rows and rows of other girls turned my skin stiff, too.

I suggested we sew a girl's coat, and Volkov loved the idea. One of his buyers, an Italian who lived in Canada ("double foreigner, double rich"), liked to spoil her daughter. As with every coat sold, we'd get a percentage of the profit. The ermine coat would earn a pretty sum. Volkov named a number high enough—in steady U.S. dollars, he assured us—to change a life, even ruin it. But the coat had to be perfect, he warned. The Italian who lived in Canada didn't just throw her money around. She bred miniature dogs, judged competitions. She could spot a blemish a continent away.

Volkov turned to me. "Her girl's about your age." His gray eyes sliced across the key points of my body: chest, waist, hips. Other men had begun looking at me this way on the streets. I'd become the sum of my chest, waist, hips—someone to be assembled. Soon I'd start wearing Aunt Milena's oversize frocks, wanting to be whole again.

That evening, when Mother pressed the tape measure to my skin, its cold metal lip made me think of Volkov. I conjured the buyer's daughter instead, soft in her ermine coat. She trudged across a snowy field, no trees or bushes around, not even a speck of dirt, nothing to mark movement except the slow crunch of her feet, and she'd better not slip and fall because no one would find her, despite her tiny flags.

Before the Union fell apart, the foreign films that made it into our country were dubbed by the same man. You could hear his dentures slap against his gums. No matter the character—man, woman, toddler—same droning voice. It flattened the characters' joy and sorrow, made us doubt their confessions. Did the heroine really love that man as much as she said? Vowing to die for him was going a bit far, wasn't it?

Sometimes the dubbing lagged so far behind, you had to guess who said what, guess how the film ended.

Volkov's buyers live around the world. Combined, they speak twenty-eight languages. I never met a single one of them, but somehow I knew they possessed that awful voice.

———

As Volkov said, the ermine coat had to be perfect: no visible seams or loose threads, the wooden claw clasps sanded by hand, lacquered without a single bubble. Normally a coat took four days to sew. This one ate up a week, two weeks. The closer Mother and Aunt Milena came to finishing the coat, the more undone they looked. Pins slipped from between their teeth. Their hands pecked at the same spot on the carpet over and over, until my sister or I found the pin for them. They seemed awake only at night, when they clattered around the kitchen chopping and frying whatever they could, mostly beets and onions. Aunt Milena would carry the ermine, a glowing bride in her arms, to the balcony, away from the smell.

How Mother and Aunt Milena met again, as told by Mother: Two years ago on her way home from work, her bus broke down near one of the villages. The next bus wasn't due for another hour, and she had to use the ladies' room. No such room was in sight, of course, only dirt fields and a few huts, their outhouses fenced off like prized bulls. Never had she relieved herself en plein air, like a brute, and she wasn't about to start now. She paced the road, every minute stretching longer and longer and her panic building, until finally she sank into a ditch, hitched up her dress, rolled down her tights, and let out a long moan. Only afterward did she realize she had nothing to wipe with. The panties she'd worn that day were more symbol than fabric, and she couldn't ruin the acorn-pattern tights she had crocheted herself, over five months, stealing time between work, chores, sleep. She would have reached for a leaf, but what was stinging nettle and what wasn't? She'd rather use the back of her own hand, then lick it clean. So she did. When she straightened up, a voice startled her from above: "Larissa?" A woman was peering into the ditch. Not just any woman, but our former neighbor—now a villager with a rake in hand and a grin so wide that Mother knew she'd witnessed all. Determined to keep a shred of dignity, Mother did what any neighbor, past or present, should do: she invited Aunt Milena over for tea.

If my mother had boarded a different bus? If she'd chosen a different ditch? She'd still be speeding by Aunt Milena's village.

The power cuts out every evening, but the moment of failure still catches me by surprise. Some secret flits between the lamps, refrigerator, television, the mixer in my mother's hand, and everything falls silent. The silence scares me more than the dark. Should we take cover, too? From what? From whom?

In our daily blind spells we've learned the geography of our apartment. The matches live two steps from the kitchen, in the bathroom cabinet, bottom shelf, but I'm not allowed to touch them anymore. The first candle: three steps down the corridor, to the left of the record player. The second candle: four steps to the right, on the windowsill by the onions sprouting from mayonnaise jars. To pass the time Aunt Milena sings folk songs she learned in the village. My sister and I belt along, garbling the Ukrainian words, understanding few of them. I had a favorite song, an especially cheery one, until Aunt Milena told me what it was about. Two Cossacks take a girl into the dark forest and tie her to a pine by her own braids and set the pine on fire— the pine burns, burns and won't go out, and the girl cries, cries and won't quiet down. After that, I want to cut off my braids but

Mother won't let me. She says I'll need them, although she won't say what for. I tuck them under my collar and never ask Aunt Milena what the words in the other songs mean.

When the coat was finished, I tried it on for the last time. The red silk lining—bought from one of Mother's old schoolmates, a urologist who also bred silkworms and therapeutic leeches—felt slippery and warm, as if the ermine had been freshly skinned. Volkov always said a good coat ought to feel like a second skin. This one became my own skin. To peel it off was painful. I'd briefly forgotten how cold the air felt, how sharp.

That evening, when my sister was safely asleep, Aunt Milena and Mother sat me down at the kitchen table, and spoke in stilted turns. They must have rehearsed who would say what. Aunt Milena: We'll use the money from the coat to get you, your sister, and your mother out of the country. Mother: They need chemists like me in the oil fields in Canada. Aunt Milena: It's so safe there, people leave their cars unlocked. (Mother, to Aunt Milena, voice low, off script: To provide pedestrians shelter from the polar bears.) (Aunt Milena, to Mother: Only in one town, up north.) Aunt Milena: Who knows, maybe one day you'll meet the girl in the ermine coat. Mother: You'll be wearing one just as lovely. Aunt Milena: Lovelier.

I asked why Aunt Milena wouldn't come with us.

"Canada will only take people who are related," Aunt Milena said, her voice suddenly hard, as if she herself had made the rules and the rules were perfectly sensible.

I waited to hear the rest of the plan.

Mother's teeth were clenched, her smile rigid.

Aunt Milena looked silently at a point above my head, maybe at an older, taller version of me, who might one day come back for a visit and thank her for letting us go, and say, "Yes, dear Aunt Milena, surely it was all for the best."

Back when we'd received our first batch of pelts, Aunt Milena had plucked a hair from one of them, held the hair over a lit match. It crackled, then burned back a few millimeters, into a neat nub.

"It smells just like burning human hair," she told me, "which smells like burning fat, only sweeter. Fake fur will stink like plastic and curl into little beads. That's how you can tell."

I remembered these words when, alone in the apartment the day after I was told about the plan, I let the flame eat away at the ermine coat. The angry fur sputtered in the bathtub, its many ermine backs arching and twisting until, all at once, with a last sigh, they gave in to the flame. Later that evening, when my mother slapped me raw, I lied and said I was only trying to see if the fur was real. It had smelled just like Aunt Milena promised.

Now and then, we still find slick black hairs on the sofa bed or on our clothes, and sometimes even a soft white hair. The hairs remind us of Volkov, the debt we owe him, as though he himself shed them for this purpose.

This is what I remember most: Before the blackouts. Before the ermine coat, before even the black coats. Aunt Milena's bag by the door, still unpacked. The four of us squeezed around the kitchen table. We had turned the lights off, lit the candles. Candlelit dinners were a luxury then. I'd learned a new song at school that day, and I taught it to my sister between forkfuls of fried cabbage. Mother got up, drew the curtains, and pulled Aunt Milena to her. As my sister and I sang, they clutched each other, tilting this way and that, as though to keep each other from falling. My sister turned to me, her face a question. "Silly," I said to her, "they're dancing."

HOMECOMING

Yet again, Zaya is returning to Internat Number 12.

Even as a nineteen-year-old, practically an adult, with a job, three changes of clothes, a new driver's license, and a rented room back in Moscow.

The *internat* closed a few years ago, its orphans released to the streets, yet here she is, hurtling toward it in a glossy black cargo van at 100 kilometers per hour. She's driving the van herself. Her own foot jerks the gas. The key to the iron gates rattles in the glove box. The key itself is iron, without a hint of rust.

The van belongs to a twenty-one-year-old heiress named Almaza Shprot. Almaza's father served as a Minister of Geology in the Soviet days, and now dabbles in the oil and gas business. Almaza owns more than three changes of clothes. In fact, if all her outfits formed a chain, cuff in cuff, and marched from her closet into the sea, the chain would never end.

Actually, Almaza's accountant would correct, the van doesn't belong to Almaza. It belongs to Almaza's company. You have to keep these things straight for tax purposes.

How the accountant classifies the company for tax purposes: TRAVEL AGENCY.

And it's true, the clients do need to travel to the company's many sites, around Russia, Latvia, and now Ukraine. But the tax forms don't have a category for the type of service the company renders once the clients arrive at their destination. Is it legal? Who knows? Certainly not a common accountant.

A better question: Is the service transformative?

Any millionaire can frolic with dolphins in Belize, catch a ballet in Paris, clear their complexion with a champagne bath, but how many can say they've feared for their lives? That they've been trampled on, reduced to nothingness, and from that nothingness been reborn? These days, in these circles—not many.

For instance, one of the company's trip packages re-creates *One Day in the Life of Ivan Denisovich*. Clients are carted out to the fringe of the Arctic Circle, to a defunct labor camp. Like the novel's protagonist, they must mop the guardhouse, lay brick walls with quick-dry mortar, fight over stone-hard bread—all this in freezing temperatures, in too-small boots, while a guard flogs them.

Almaza likes to experience the sites along with the clients. "Ivan Denisovich had one bad day, and got a whole memoir out of it," Almaza tells them. "Imagine the creative possibilities."

"I don't think it was just one day," an aluminum tycoon remarks, but nobody hears him through the burlap potato sack wrapped over his mouth and nose.

By the time the clients return to Moscow, dirty and bruised, they're ready to kiss the leather of their cars, kiss their drivers, even—grateful for any simple pleasure.

—

As an employee of the company, Zaya wears many hats. Depending on the trip package, she's the interrogator or torturer or prison guard, or some combination of the three.

Zaya has considered quitting. It's as demeaning for her to play the villain as it is for the clients to play victim—maybe more. But who else would hire Zaya, with that mean mangled lip? Her face screams knife fight. Gang affiliation. She'd have to go back to selling cigarette butts at the bazaar, where the company recruiter originally discovered her. And, loath as she is to admit it, she's good at this job. Better than her predecessors. She can distinguish between the shades of horror in her victims' faces, knows just how far to push until the victims reveal their most vulnerable spots, their deepest fears. When Zaya thinks back on it, wreaking terror has always been her specialty. As early as age six: one evening after she'd run away from the *internat* and the boot maker took her in, Zaya let a candle tip, watched the flames lap at the lace curtains. Zaya knew the boot maker wouldn't let her stay for long anyway, so why not let the flames climb, speed up the parting?

"What's the most intimate act between people?" Almaza once mused in Zaya's presence, leafing through a dog-eared porn magazine she'd found under a prison mattress. The throes of pleasure Zaya glimpsed inside resembled torment. "If not sex, then kissing?" asked Almaza.

Every time a client submits to Zaya, she wants to tell Almaza: "It's this."

"The child who is not embraced by the village will burn it down to feel its warmth." Almaza had been quoting her favorite African proverb while puttering at the Chernobyl site. She was chucking bits of concrete into a wheelbarrow, her paper hazmat suit crinkling.

The company hadn't been able to get clearance to use the real Chernobyl—and anyway, the real Chernobyl was looking too tidy these days, with the sarcophagus the French and Germans were erecting over it—so the site was a decommissioned reactor in Latvia. None of the clients seemed to mind.

Zaya urged on the cleanup crew as their faux radiation gauges beeped. They had to shovel sand over any debris they couldn't lift. One woman, a TV personality with cherry lipstick still caked in the corners of her mouth, fell to her knees in exhaustion. Zaya bent close to the woman's grimy face, considered her wide dark eyes. "Want pretty blue eyes instead?" she offered, her voice sickly sweet. "I'll reassign you to Reactor Four. The radiation inside is so high, I hear it does wonders." The woman stood up, knees shaking.

"My problem?" Almaza went on. "I was embraced too tightly as a child." Her parents had loved her in a simple, predictable way, giving her everything she wanted. As a result, she didn't have the capacity to do anything as poetic as burn down a village.

Almaza turned to Zaya, as though remembering that she had been a child once, too. "Where did you grow up?"

Zaya told her.

"How awful," Almaza whimpered. "Just dreadful." And then, gleeful: "I can't imagine a worse place."

Is this where Zaya went wrong? Is it because she evoked for Almaza the tall iron fence, the dark cavernous halls of the monastery, is this how she is being reeled back in now?

But maybe, even if she hadn't told Almaza about the *internat,* she'd be driving along this gravel road just the same, drawn in by some other conspiracy of circumstances. She can't escape the *internat*'s magnetic pull. It must be fated, like the lifelong slide toward death.

After hearing about Zaya's childhood, Almaza said: "What you need to do is harness all that authentic trauma into something great. A waste of trauma not to." She suggested Zaya could invent a raw new dance style. Immortalize her woes in a brutal tile mural. She could write a memoir.

"Just look at that other orphan, the one all over the news," Almaza reminded Zaya. The girl had grown up in an *internat* like Zaya's, and couldn't walk. Not that it stopped her from dreaming. She got herself adopted by a Finnish philanthropist, endured ten spinal surgeries, regained a bit of feeling in her right leg, and became a Paralympic gymnast. Inspired the whole country. She even posed for a beauty magazine, her long legs model thin.

Upon arrival at the *internat*, Zaya is disappointed to find the place intact. Even though she'd been absent for a short three years, she'd imagined coming upon a pile of bricks and plaster, impossible to reassemble. But the building stands; lush vines seal its cracks, cushion the iron fence. The vines shroud the mounds where the children were buried, and the unfilled pits, too—a relief, for Zaya. As a child, she had feared being mistaken for dead, waking up buried in one of these pits.

Now the grounds look charming, with the buttercups dotting the wild grass, the gates thrown open in welcome.

The clients—a venture capitalist, a socialite, a steel magnate, a lifestyle manager—are due to arrive the next morning. In preparation Zaya oils the gates' locks, mops the floors, stocks the canteen with food, straightens the rows of beds in the nave of the monastery. Cold, dim, with spider egg sacs suspended in the stone moldings, the hall still possesses an underground quality.

Zaya tries to remember which bed was hers. To pass the time as a child she'd stand on her bed, use a sharp rock to scratch open the tight-lipped mouths of the men frescoed on the walls. But it appears that other children took up the practice after her time: now every mouth within reach is agape, as if the painted figures are shocked to find themselves, after so many centuries, in the same stultifying place.

Roaming the chambers and corridors, Zaya feels a sudden absence on her hip, as though something has been carved from her side. She recalls she used to carry the mummified saint, in a pillowcase propped on her hip, not because she wanted its companionship day and night—the creature smelled like a stale dishrag—but to keep the other children from stealing it, yanking its hair.

In the back of the building, Zaya discovers a small cell-like room with bare plaster walls and an adult-size bed, likely for a *sanitarka*. She rolls out a sleeping bag. The thin straw mattress, ripping at the seams, is just as hard as the ones on the children's beds.

What about that other famous orphan, Almaza has reminded Zaya. When that girl's orphanage ran out of money, the *sanitarki* chopped off the children's braids and sold them to an Italian wig maker. Virgin hair, untouched by chemicals or curling irons. So what did this girl do when she got out? She started her own wig-making business, and partnered with a temple in India where the women cede their braids by choice, as an offering. Almaza herself owned one of these wigs back in Moscow. Finely woven, by three-strand bunches. It cost her fifteen thousand USD for one wig. Now the orphan drives a nice car, owns an apartment with French doors.

What does Zaya think of that? What's Zaya's excuse for her life?

The next day, a silver SUV deposits Almaza and the clients at the *internat*. Two men and two women, not including Almaza. The men are fleshy, grayish, the women tall and narrow with cinched, dehydrated looks. As instructed, everyone wears sensible shoes.

Zaya wears a white *sanitarka* dress—or rather, the company designer's interpretation of that uniform: a sculpted top half, double-breasted, vaguely military, with a long billowing skirt that drags in the wild grass, collecting spiny seeds.

After ushering the group into the courtyard and locking the gates behind them, Zaya orders everyone to make a line in front of her. Almaza, orphan-chic in her long black pigtails, distressed jeans, and threadbare cotton shirt, asks, "Make a line by height, net worth, or . . . ?"

"By age," Zaya improvises. "Oldest at the back."

But no one wants to admit their age, not even Almaza, who hardly looks older than Zaya. One of the clients, a leggy socialite whose tanned skin appears poreless, jokes with the group that she is ageless—her two pregnancies only made her look better, not worse. The clients shuffle on the spot until Zaya threatens to sort them herself, using the dates of birth on the IDs they submitted.

At last, everyone in a crooked formation, Zaya distributes to each client the single garment for their ten-day stay, as well as a garbage bag for their clothes, wallets, and other personal effects. They won't have access to their belongings until they leave, Zaya reminds them.

The clients take turns changing in the outdoor shower (out of service, they will soon discover). When the men and women reconvene in the courtyard, looking like a bridal party in their matching periwinkle frocks, they place their garbage bags at Zaya's feet.

"Phones, too," Zaya tells the impeccably postured lifestyle manager, who clutches a handset, the latest model. With a sigh the woman presses the phone against her hip to retract the telescopic antenna, then thrusts the bulky device into Zaya's outstretched hand.

The clients await further instruction.

Zaya hasn't thought of anything beyond this part. Usually Almaza supplies her with an itinerary of activities. But now, Almaza is regarding her with the same excited obedience as the others.

A nightingale sings from a nearby bush. A butterfly circles the steel magnate's parched knee.

Zaya struggles to remember how the *sanitarki* would entertain the children. Her mind leaps over long expanses of formless time. She slings the garbage bags over her shoulder and follows the brick path toward the arched entrance of the building, hoping for an idea along the way. The group trails her. She hears the steel magnate remark, "A shame this place closed down."

—

Apart from setting out food at mealtimes (a vat of rehydrated sea cabbage, with a tube of liver paste) and restocking the latrine with toilet paper (newspaper), Zaya keeps to her room. She lies in bed, blinking at the low vaulted ceiling. Like the clients, she came here expecting to feel something. Instead, she has found her senses dulled.

Maybe it's because she knows the escape hatch.

Or at least, the possibility of one.

She knows she could walk the 25 kilometers to Kirovka and stay with Konstantyn. Three months ago she saw a photo of him in a newspaper, standing in front of his apartment block, arms crossed. He'd bought up an additional suite, the article informed her, which he converted into a tomb for the saint.

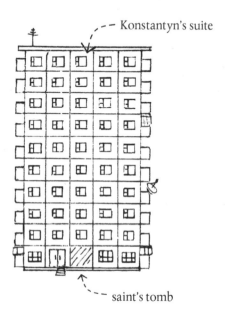

Konstantyn's suite

saint's tomb

"He's ruining the neighborhood," commented Lila Palash-kina, 73, longtime tenant. "All these noisy fanatics, crowding in."

"The saint and I are not going anywhere," responded Konstantyn Illych Boyko, 50, business owner and poet, none of whose books remain in print.

White-haired with dark bulges under his eyes, he had looked tired in the photo, and much older than the last time Zaya had seen him. The building didn't look great either, blotchy, riddled with cracks. She wished for a photo of the saint as well, just to see it again; the article had mentioned a linen sheet covering the saint, and said that the tomb's guard refused to remove it.

If Konstantyn had taken Zaya in before, surely he wouldn't object to her presence now, for another day or two? Another expended bowl of pork stew, lusciously greasy? She could use him like he'd once used her. So long as she considered it a simple transaction, not a favor, she could let herself knock on his door.

"Maybe this is the point," the clients whisper outside Zaya's window on the second morning. "Maybe we're supposed to feel abandoned."

They take the initiative, find their own ordeals.

"That grassy knoll?" says the stocky venture capitalist, pointing. "To the invalids who lived here, it must have seemed a mountain." He braids wild grass into ropes, with which he ties thick branches to the sides of his legs, rendering his knees unbendable.

"A few of the orphans might have never even seen it." The socialite rips a strip off the bottom of her frock, blindfolds herself.

The steel magnate plugs his ears with poplar fluff.
Almaza fills her boots with gravel.

On the third morning, when setting out the latrine newspaper
(one broadsheet per day), Zaya comes upon a second article
about Konstantyn and the tomb, published a week ago.

The saint's tomb had caved in, the article reports. Sheets of
vinyl flooring, rugs, furniture, appliances, hot-water radiators,
framed photographs, toys, a porcelain dish set, jars of fermented
tomatoes—all this piled into the tomb from the apartment
above, along with a family of three, shocked but unharmed,
their mouths, allegedly, still full of breakfast. Luckily, that morning the tomb was closed, its live-in guard having been fired for
undisclosed reasons.

"Must be the shifting earth, the encroaching marshes,"
commented Konstantyn Illych Boyko, who had failed to insure
his business and, the newspaper noted, had also failed in
marriage.

"Must be those inner walls Konstantyn Illych knocked out,"
stated the former guard, who had been intercepted at the train
station on his way to Kiev, where he would seek employment
in customer service. The man, endowed with impeccably white
teeth, wished to remain anonymous.

Zaya examines the accompanying photo. She wonders if
the apartment block is wide enough for the rest of the structure
to remain sound.

"You might want to clear out," Almaza tells Zaya from the
doorway of the latrine. She has tied an off-center knot at the
hem of her frock, for a fitted faux-slit look. "I slipped laxatives
into the clients' breakfast. Dysentery day."

On the fourth evening at the *internat,* visitors start emerging from the forest, crowding the iron gates. Three at first, then five more follow. Most are around Zaya's age. Among the visitors is a teenage boy, orange-maned, laden with a tattered gym bag. His right eye is pressed deeper into his head than the left. He tells Zaya that he and the others had grown up at the *internat,* and heard it was reopening. They'd been living on the streets, and now they want back in. When Zaya tries to turn them away, the boy says, "But we walked all the way here." They'd started at sunrise, and now it was almost sundown. They'd been stalked by a wild boar, dive-bombed by crows. A bunch of them had turned back already. "But we made it," the boy insists.

Before this job, Zaya herself had been living on the streets, in Moscow's labyrinthine suburbs, huddling up to the warm aboveground pipes that fed wastewater from power plants to household radiators. "I'm sorry," Zaya says, but she isn't. She wants these visitors to go away. It's as if the *internat* is rebuilding itself, and soon the real *sanitarki* will return, a director will materialize.

A round-faced woman among the crowd at the gates smooths her dirty wrinkled blouse over her stomach, as if the blouse is the problem. She points toward Almaza and the clients, who are limping around the courtyard with their legs in splints, pebbles spilling from their shoes. "But you let *them* in."

"They paid to be here."

The group awaits an explanation.

After a pause, Zaya says, "I don't understand it either."

"Hey," says the woman in the wrinkled blouse, "I remember you."

On second look, Zaya remembers the woman, too, but she feigns ignorance. As a girl, this woman used to follow the *sanitarki* around, asking for the tips of their braids to make into hair dolls. Now the woman has a pair of thin braids of her own, wispy ends dusting her shoulders. Zaya, on the other hand, has kept her hair buzzed; any time it grows out, the strands feel like fingers on her nape, threatening to stretch around her neck.

"How'd you get to be a *sanitarka*?" asks a man with pink heart-shaped glasses too small for his face. Despite the bushy beard, Zaya recognizes him as well.

"I'm not a real one," Zaya says, more forcefully than she'd intended.

The clients are not yet asking for their money back, exactly, but would any of them recommend the place? Of all the other trips the company offers? Sure, the child-size beds are lumpy, the food lousy, the latrines reek, but no one has been properly traumatized. No one is falling apart or pulling themselves back together. And despite efforts to keep busy, the past four days have been downright dull.

It's also awkward for the clients to be forced to look at all those sad people loitering at the gates. More and more keep showing up. They sleep under sagging tarps. How many now, fifteen? Can't Zaya get rid of them? It doesn't help that Almaza barters with them through the gates. She trades slices of the liver paste for their coffee, fresh off their camping stove. She sighs at them in regret. "Honey," she tells the teenager with the pressed-in eye, "if only we could trade places."

On the fifth day, when Zaya sets out moldy bread and rancid margarine for breakfast, the clients don't show up. Zaya scopes out the building and the sunny meadow behind it, calling Almaza's name.

"Over here!" Almaza's hoarse voice reaches Zaya from the grassy knoll—seemingly, from deep inside it.

Zaya rounds the knoll to discover Almaza and all four clients crouching in a narrow, weed-strewn hole, looking small and scared. The hole is just deep enough to trap them. "What took you so long? We were calling for you all night," Almaza says, hugging her knees to her chest, her long black ponytail draped around her neck like a scarf. The venture capitalist and steel magnate have their arms wrapped around each other. The lifestyle manager picks at a crown of wilted dandelions atop the socialite's head.

"Is this one of the graves you told me about?" asks Almaza. "The to-be-filled ones?"

"They were never this deep," says Zaya.

"This one wasn't deep, at first, either." Almaza had stumbled into a shallow pit, everyone else had followed, and the ground beneath them caved in. "There are tunnels down here. We've been crawling around, trying to find a way out." Her face strains; she's on the verge of tears. "We could've been eaten by an animal. Or by a hundred spiders, whose venom would slowly predigest us. Something could've happened to you, and we'd be stuck here for days and days until our drivers found our hollowed corpses." As she lists all the ghastly scenarios, the clients nod along, gasping as one might do when presented with an exotic restaurant menu. Almaza delights in her performance, gesticulates wildly in the cramped space. She takes a dramatic pause. "We'd be like the orphans who died here, buried en masse."

Zaya glares at the clients, suddenly enraged.

She spots a rusty shovel leaning against the wall of the monastery, and uses it to fling a fist-size clod of dirt into the pit. It explodes against the socialite's knee. Almaza and the clients squeal in mock horror.

Next comes an entire shovelful. The venture capitalist receives the earth spilling over his bald head with rapture, as if it were holy water.

The lifestyle manager moans with pleasure. "I vow to quit my job, take up painting again."

The steel magnate shouts above them all, "I vow to get my wife and kids back."

The earth grows soft, welcoming Zaya's shovel. There's a rhythm to the slicing, the earth landing with a soft thud. She finds herself counting each stroke. Now the squeals of the clients are turning into screams, but she doesn't stop, doesn't break the rhythm. Her anger has ebbed, and is replaced by a logistical curiosity, cold and foreign: How many strokes to fill the pit? She stabs at a weedy ledge and the entire thing comes away, triggers a slide of earth and rocks. The clients try to scramble to their feet but are knocked back down. When the slide settles, they are buried to the chest. Zaya lifts the shovel again; her need to restart the rhythm, the pulse, is dire, desperate—as though her own heart has stopped. Five dirty tear-streaked faces tilt up in a childlike stupor. For a moment Zaya wonders whether they are looking not at her but at some wrathful deity behind her, capable only of destroying.

And yet Almaza says, "Oh, Zaya." Her voice is awed, naked, and she breaks into a smile. "Couldn't have planned it better myself."

"The adrenaline," whispers the steel magnate.

"We'll spruce up these graves," Almaza declares, slowly at first. "We'll make a maze of the tunnels, for more clients. We'll fix up your room, have you live here like you own the place." Almaza wrenches her arms from the dirt, shakes out her ponytail. "Technically you already own it. I bought the *internat* in your name."

Zaya feels dizzy, as though sun-stricken. "You did not."

"Did so. As a foreigner I'd have to pay an extra tax."

The shovel in Zaya's hands feels unbearably heavy. Does it, too, belong to her?

Apparently, wreaking terror is all Zaya is good for. Had she forgotten? She thinks of the boot maker again. After the hut had burned down and the woman had delivered Zaya back to the orphanage—this same woman who had found her on the forest floor, gasping for breath, with yellowed eyes and a slit lip that made Zaya look, the woman told her, like a fish dragged from the sea until the hook dislodged; this same woman who had carried Zaya in her arms and nursed her back to health—the abandonment hadn't hurt. Zaya had felt numb. She hadn't let herself dream of living with the boot maker. Nor had Zaya, many years later, imagined living with Konstantyn. When she'd spat on the Party members at the pageant, she'd also spat on the possibility (however slim) of a home back in Kirovka. The *internat* had taught her well: as soon as you want something, you lack it; and if you do get it, it can easily be taken away. But this lesson came at a cost—a dry unfeeling clump had formed in her chest, had grown with age. She wonders now: If she slit her skin open, would nothing but sawdust spill out?

Down in the pit, the clients are bickering.

The venture capitalist asks Almaza why she bought the monastery instead of leasing it. Almaza tells him she doesn't like leasing things. Does she lease the penthouse she sleeps in? The jewelry she wears? The meals she eats?

Zaya considers. She can fill the pit, finish them all off. She has no doubt now she is capable of this. Tantalized, she has unlocked a secret chamber within herself, discovered its horrors.

She drops the shovel, backs away.

"Where do you think you're going?" Almaza calls from the pit. "Get us out."

The soiled skirt of her white dress bunched under one arm, Zaya crosses the grounds like a runaway bride. She heaves open the iron gates, steps between the orphans sleeping on the dewy grass, still waiting to be let in. She climbs into the black cargo van and honks the horn, waking the campers.

"Get in," she calls from her rolled-down window. "We're getting out of here, for good."

The campers squint at her sleepily. The orange-maned teenager props himself up on his elbows, nods toward the gates. "She left it open," he tells the others.

"Don't even try," Zaya warns. "Get in or I'm rolling over you."

"Where are you taking us?" asks the teenager.

Zaya thinks on it. "Wherever you were before."

No one moves.

"You get fired?" asks the woman with the wispy braids, adjusting her rucksack under her head.

"I'm trying to help you." Zaya is unsure, precisely, how. She slumps in her seat, suddenly exhausted.

"Does anyone else hear the screaming?" asks the man with heart-shaped glasses.

"I bet if you grow your hair out you'll get another job," the teenager says to Zaya, smiling shyly.

The others study Zaya's face, her botched lip, and keep silent.

Zaya backs the van onto the road in a swift arc, hoping to make plain her threat of leaving them behind. She begins to roll away, glancing in the rearview mirror, expecting the campers to jolt up, pile into the van with their tents and tarps and camping stoves. But they don't. One by one, they walk in the other direction, enter the gates.

The rest of the drive is a breathless full-throttle dash, Zaya narrowly making the curves in the road. This deep dread is what freedom feels like, she tells herself. She feels it every time she runs away.

She imagines what she'll tell Konstantyn. This stolen van is all she has to show for herself, unlike the superorphans Almaza is always raving about. Zaya hasn't remade her life into an inspiring lesson, hasn't grown rich or famous—and literally, she hasn't grown at all. Perhaps the fact that she remains small will also be a disappointment.

Kirovka looks more ratty than Zaya remembers it, its roads cratered, its lamp poles a drunken procession leaning in every direction. Only the banks and pharmacies appear new—almost every block has one or the other—their respective aprons of sidewalk freshly tiled. Zaya weaves along the town's streets, searching for Konstantyn's building. In the center of the tree-lined plaza, she spots a concrete pedestal, from the old Lenin statue. Only his feet remain now, big as bathtubs, rusty rebar curving from them like veins.

At last Zaya parks in front of 1933 Ivansk.

She beholds the sight, trying to make sense of it. Konstantyn's tenth-floor suite—she recognizes the red-and-white-checkered curtains—is the last left hanging intact between two pillars of rubble. She can see cornflower-blue sky through a gap in the center. The edifice seems, understandably, abandoned.

Still, Zaya calls his name.

A piece of debris flakes off Konstantyn's apartment, hurtles to the ground, and smashes into a fine dust.

Zaya doesn't know if it is hope, or the devastating absence of it, that makes her take a step toward the building.

Another step, tentative, as if she is approaching a sleeping bear.

Once inside, though, she bounds up the dusty staircase. An unsettling draft blows through the many cracks in the walls. A pair of roaches the size of her hand skitter down a dark corridor—no, surely just rats?—but still she climbs.

When she reaches Suite 76—its steel outer door freckled

Konstantyn's suite

with rust—she lifts the heavy knocker and raps. After a moment she hears the click of the inner door's dead bolt. A familiar sound—yet under the circumstances, miraculous. She hears the inner door squeal open—its red faux-leather upholstery surfaces in her mind—then the ticking of more locks, like clockwork, followed by the gravelly melody of the chain sliding along its track, and dropping. At last the steel door swings open.

For a moment Konstantyn stands there, blinking, a dripping wooden spoon in hand.

He doesn't look at her with fear, as the clients did, but regards her with simple recognition. She feels herself shrinking, suddenly powerless, but also—with relief—less monstrous.

"Just in time for lunch," Konstantyn announces. His eyes flit over her billowy white dress but, mercifully, he doesn't ask questions. He steps aside to let her in, as if she's just returned from a stroll, as if he'd been expecting her.

The smell of the apartment greets her, unchanged. Old books, laurel leaves. A pot of soup bubbles on the stove, infusing the air with a sharp sweetness, like the underbelly of a rotting log. Zaya can't recall the last time she ate.

"Mushroom soup," he exclaims, as though nothing could make him happier. He gestures to a chair at the kitchen table.

The fact that the apartment hangs above an abyss becomes a distant worry.

The soup is salty but delicious, globs of oil shimmering over fungal caps and gills. She remembers not to scoop her spoon too deep, where the peppercorns hide. As she devours two bowlfuls with three slices of rye bread, uncertain if she'll be invited to stay for another meal, Konstantyn chatters away. The other tenants having evacuated, he's never lived in such quiet, he tells her. He thought he'd enjoy it, but at night he can hear his own pulse, like the drum of an approaching army. A few tenants moved to their dachas, others moved in with relatives many towns over. His ex-wife, whom he hopes Zaya might one day meet, left for Poland with her new family—he pauses at this last word, a seemingly difficult verdict.

"What happened to the saint?" Zaya asks. She wants to keep him talking as she reaches for more bread.

Observing how Konstantyn's face darkens, she senses that his chatter has been an effort to avoid the subject.

"I'm so sorry. The saint is gone," he says at last. "But at least it wasn't crushed under the rubble." A few days before the tomb caved in, Konstantyn discovered that the guard had sold the saint. When he demanded the saint's return, the guard told him it would be impossible, the saint could be anywhere. "Actually, *everywhere*," Konstantyn corrects himself. "It had been split into many pieces."

Zaya smiles at this thought, imagines the saint scattered all over the Earth, ever present. Satiated at last, she slips her half-eaten piece of bread into a pocket for later. "Why didn't you leave like the others?" she asks. "Go to your dacha?"

"I've been busy." His face erupts in a grin. "Home renovation. I've squeezed in a second room," he says. "Yours."

Konstantyn nods at a cherrywood door off the corridor. Zaya doesn't remember it being there before. He springs to his feet, beckons her over, opens it. They stand at the threshold.

In the years to come, Zaya will reminisce about this room. It's truly beautiful, everything she hadn't dared dream of as a child, and it will stretch larger and larger in her mind, hold more windows. She'll remember the telescope, the easel. The bronze gilded wallpaper and the painted sun shining from the ceiling, its rays twirling ribbons. The books, spines uncracked, take up an entire wall of shelves. Most of all she'll remember Konstantyn, beaming at her. "Welcome home."

She won't know, won't want to know, which of these remembered details are real.

She gets only a glimpse of her new room before its glossy hardwood floor gives out.

The furniture folds into the center of the room and vanishes, like a pop-up card closing.

One of the walls falls away, pulling a chunk of ceiling along with it. Zaya watches books flutter ten stories down, like a dole of doves.

For a second she thinks she could stay here until the entire apartment succumbs, but her body instinctively snaps into action. She grabs Konstantyn's hand and pulls him back through the corridor. Light floods in as the walls and the rest of the ceiling crumble behind them. They race down the staircase two steps at a time, terrified of tripping, more terrified of slowing down. At last they're outside, across the road.

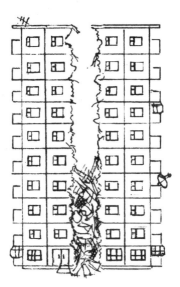

Konstantyn doubles over, panting. A deafening crack, and the two halves of the building tumble into each other like lovers reunited, then collapse. A great plume of dust envelops them.

With each passing year Zaya thinks, Perhaps just one more year? The place isn't so bad, after all. The Church has restored the cupolas, sealed the scratches in the frescoes and repainted them. Zaya keeps the *sanitarka* room, and Konstantyn sleeps in the sun-warmed attic. It was his idea to lease the monastery to the Church, after he and Zaya ate through the sea cabbage and squeezed flat the last tube of liver paste.

After 1933 Ivansk collapsed, Zaya had returned to the monastery with Konstantyn riding in the van's passenger seat. They found the place deserted, the orphans and clients gone. The orphans must have pulled the screaming clients out of the hole—not just a hole to the orphans, but a grave yawning open. The only things left behind were the papers attesting to Zaya's ownership of the property, thrown onto her bed. Zaya had imagined Almaza casting a last wary gaze over the lush grounds, their beauty having revealed a shameful secret.

Now Zaya wanders the meadows, watching the bustling monks as they hike up their robes to pull weeds. They try to fill in all the pits, but the property is large, and it isn't unusual to stumble upon yet another unfilled hole. They've torn down that old fence, and soon will build an even taller, sturdier one. For security. The forest is full of beasts, the monks say. We've got to keep them out.

ACKNOWLEDGMENTS

My deepest gratitude to those who helped bring this book into the world: Amelia (Molly) Atlas, agent extraordinaire and short-story advocate. Everyone at Doubleday, especially Lee Boudreaux for her unifying vision for this book. At Knopf Canada, Lynn Henry for her wisdom and willingness to dive into the weeds of the sentences with me, and Rick Meier, who played a key role when the book was on submission. Heartfelt thanks to Sarah Savitt and Donna Coonan at Virago Books, as well as Charlotte Stroomer and Jack Smyth for the cover.

I owe a debt of gratitude to the Michener Center for Writers for giving me the time, resources, and mentorship to write this book. Special thanks to Elizabeth McCracken, Deb Olin Unferth, Jim Magnuson, Steven Dietz, Edward Carey, Bret Anthony Johnston, Michael Adams, Ben Fountain, Marla Akin, Debbie Dewees, Billy Fatzinger, and Holly Doyel. Thank you, Lara Prescott, Olga Vilkotskaya, Jessica Topacio Long, Nouri Zarrugh, Veronica Martin—invaluable classmates and friends. Thanks as well to Zoey Leigh Peterson and Julie Wernersbach, and to benefactors from the underworld: James A. Michener and E. L. Keene.

The writing community of Vancouver, especially Renée Sarojini Saklikar, whose mentorship came at a crucial time, and

Isaac Yuen, for his friendship and exquisite prose. The Writers' Trust of Canada and RBC Bank, for the generous support. Adam Day at the Baltic Writing Residency, where the "Lucky Toss" story unlocked itself at last.

The editors and journals who first published these stories: C. Michael Curtis at *The Atlantic*, Claire Boyle at *McSweeney's*, Rosalind Porter at *Granta*.

Huge appreciation to my parents, Jane and Alex, for their unwavering support. This book began with a lunchtime conversation about our old building in Ukraine (also missing from municipal records). I've gone back to that building many times to make sure it still stands. But maybe it was never really there?

Much gratitude to my grandfather Georgiy Reva, a well of historical and literary knowledge.

To Little Jerry, for standing guard.

To Michael, for everything. To Michael's parents, for their curiosity, openness, and kindness.

And thank you, forever, to my sister Anna Pidgorna, first reader and confidante, who gave me the courage to write. This book is for you.